cul de sac

(a chloe fine psychological suspense—book 3)

blake pierce

ISBN: 978-1-64029-769-2

BOOKS BY BLAKE PIERCE

A JESSIE HUNT PSYCHOLOGICAL SUSPENSE SERIES
THE PERFECT WIFE (Book #1)
THE PERFECT BLOCK (Book #2)
THE PERFECT HOUSE (Book #3)
THE PERFECT SMILE (Book #4)

CHLOE FINE PSYCHOLOGICAL SUSPENSE SERIES
NEXT DOOR (Book #1)
A NEIGHBOR'S LIE (Book #2)
CUL DE SAC (Book #3)
SILENT NEIGHBOR (Book 34)

KATE WISE MYSTERY SERIES
IF SHE KNEW (Book #1)
IF SHE SAW (Book #2)
IF SHE RAN (Book #3)
IF SHE HID (Book #4)
IF SHE FLED (Book #5)

THE MAKING OF RILEY PAIGE SERIES
WATCHING (Book #1)
WAITING (Book #2)
LURING (Book #3)
TAKING (Book #4)

RILEY PAIGE MYSTERY SERIES
ONCE GONE (Book #1)
ONCE TAKEN (Book #2)
ONCE CRAVED (Book #3)
ONCE LURED (Book #4)
ONCE HUNTED (Book #5)
ONCE PINED (Book #6)
ONCE FORSAKEN (Book #7)
ONCE COLD (Book #8)
ONCE STALKED (Book #9)
ONCE LOST (Book #10)
ONCE BURIED (Book #11)
ONCE BOUND (Book #12)
ONCE TRAPPED (Book #13)

ONCE DORMANT (Book #14)
ONCE SHUNNED (Book #15)

MACKENZIE WHITE MYSTERY SERIES
BEFORE HE KILLS (Book #1)
BEFORE HE SEES (Book #2)
BEFORE HE COVETS (Book #3)
BEFORE HE TAKES (Book #4)
BEFORE HE NEEDS (Book #5)
BEFORE HE FEELS (Book #6)
BEFORE HE SINS (Book #7)
BEFORE HE HUNTS (Book #8)
BEFORE HE PREYS (Book #9)
BEFORE HE LONGS (Book #10)
BEFORE HE LAPSES (Book #11)
BEFORE HE ENVIES (Book #12)

AVERY BLACK MYSTERY SERIES
CAUSE TO KILL (Book #1)
CAUSE TO RUN (Book #2)
CAUSE TO HIDE (Book #3)
CAUSE TO FEAR (Book #4)
CAUSE TO SAVE (Book #5)
CAUSE TO DREAD (Book #6)

KERI LOCKE MYSTERY SERIES
A TRACE OF DEATH (Book #1)
A TRACE OF MUDER (Book #2)
A TRACE OF VICE (Book #3)
A TRACE OF CRIME (Book #4)
A TRACE OF HOPE (Book #5)

PROLOGUE

Jerry Hilyard pulled his Mercedes Benz into his driveway just after one o'clock on a Monday afternoon and smiled wide. There was nothing better than owning your own business and being rich enough to call it a day whenever you wanted.

Jerry looked forward to the look of surprise on his wife's face when he told her he was taking her out for a surprise lunch. He wanted to make it a brunch, but he knew Lauren would still be nursing a hangover from the night before. She had stayed out way too late, going, for reasons he still did not understand, to her twenty-year high school reunion. By lunchtime, she should be less cranky—and maybe even up for joining him for a Bloody Mary or two.

He smiled when he thought of the good news that he would be sharing with her: he was planning a two-week getaway to Greece. Just him and her, without the kids. They'd be leaving next month.

Jerry walked to the door, briefcase in hand, excited about how the afternoon might turn out. He found the door locked, which wasn't unusual. She had never been a trusting sort of woman, even in a neighborhood as well-to-do as theirs.

As he unlocked the door and made his way into the kitchen to pour himself a glass of wine, he realized that he could not hear the bedroom television. The house was just as quiet as when he had left. Maybe the hangover had not yet run its course.

He wondered how the reunion had gone last night. She hadn't really spoken about it that morning. He had been in her same graduating class but he *loathed* sentimental nonsense like high school reunions. All it was at its core was an excuse for classmates to get together ten or twenty years later to see who was doing better than everyone else. But once Lauren's friends had convinced her to go, she'd gotten almost excited about seeing some of her old classmates. Or so it had seemed. The intake of alcohol last night indicated that it might have been a rough night all around.

These thoughts were parading through Jerry's head as he made his way through the upstairs hallway toward their bedroom. But as he neared the doorway, he stopped.

It was very quiet.

Sure, this was to be expected if Lauren was indeed taking a nap and had not put on Netflix to finish binging whichever show had been her fancy for the week. But this was a different kind of quiet…a total lack of movement or motion that seemed out of place. It was like a silence he could hear—a silence he could literally *feel*.

Something's wrong, he thought.

It was a frightening thought but still, he moved toward the door quickly. He had to know, had to make sure…

Make sure what?

All he saw at first was red. On the bedsheets, on the walls, a dark red so thick and dark that it was almost black in places.

A scream pushed itself up through his lungs and out of his mouth. He didn't know if he should go running to her or downstairs to the phone.

In the end, he did neither. His legs gave out and the weight of his gut-wrenching screams took him to the floor, where he pounded his fists, where he tried to make sense of the horrific sight in front of him.

CHAPTER ONE

Chloe focused, narrowed her vision down the sight of the gun, and fired.

The recoil was gentle, the blast light and almost peaceful to her. She breathed deeply and fired again. It was easy; it came naturally to her now.

She could not see the target at the other end of the indoor range, but she knew she'd made two good shots. She was able to get a sense about these things lately. It was one of the ways she knew she was growing into the position as an agent. She was more comfortable with the sidearm, the stock and the trigger as familiar as her own hands when she could really get into the zone. In the past, she'd gone to the range only as a study of sorts, a way to improve and get better. But now, she enjoyed it. There was freedom to it, a weird release from firing at even just a paper target.

God knew she needed to feel that way as of late.

It had been a lackluster two weeks at work, leaving Chloe with nothing much to do but assisting others with data and research work. She'd nearly been pulled in to help a team with a small-time hacking sting and she'd been far too excited about it. It made her realize just how slow things had been for her as of late.

That's how she ended up at the range. It wasn't necessarily her ideal way to pass the time, but she knew she needed some practice. While she had been among the best in her class on her way through the academy, being transitioned from the Evidence Response Team to the Violent Crimes Program had made her realize that she could never be too sharp, too on top of her game.

As she fired off several more rounds into a target fifty yards away, she understood how people were drawn to it. You were absolutely alone, just you and your firearm and a target in the sights. There was something very Zen about it, the focus and the intent behind it. And then there was the *pop* of the gunshot in the open space. The one thing Chloe had always taken away from her time at the range was just how fluid the relationship between the human body and a sidearm could be. When focused, her Glock felt like a simple extension of her arm, something else she could control with her mind in the same way she controlled the movements of her fingers or arms. It was a cautionary example of how her gun should only be used when absolutely necessary because when you are trained to use it, it can start to feel almost *too* natural to squeeze the trigger.

When her session was over, she collected her targets and took stock. She had a surprising number of direct hits to the center of the target but a few stragglers to the outside, right along the edges of the paper.

She took a few pictures of the targets with her phone and made a few notes, ensuring that she would improve next time. She then tossed the paper targets and made her way out of the facility. As she did, she felt yet another thing that she assumed was so appealing to those who spent a great deal of time at the range. The feeling of numerous recoils thrumming through her hands and wrists felt peculiar, yet at the same time, pleasant in a way she could not quite describe.

As she made her way out through the lobby, she saw a familiar face coming through the door. It was Kyle Moulton, the man who had been assigned as her partner but also a man she had not seen much of over the last few weeks due to the slow caseload. She had a moment of school-girl panic when Moulton flashed a smile at her as the doors closed behind her.

"Agent Fine," he said, with an almost sarcastic tone. They knew each other well enough to drop the *Agent* and just use first names. In fact, Chloe was certain there was some romantic tension brewing between them. She'd felt it on her end almost right away, from the moment she had seen him to the moment they had wrapped their first case three months ago.

"Agent Moulton," she responded in kind.

"Blowing off steam or just passing the time?" he asked.

"A bit of both," she said. "I'm just feeling restless lately, you know?"

"I do. Riding a desk doesn't seem to do it for me, either. But…well, I didn't know you frequented the gun range."

"Just trying to stay sharp."

"I see," he said, smiling.

The silence that fell on them was the typical one that Chloe was getting used to. She hated to feel so conceited, but she was fairly certain he was feeling the same thing she was feeling. It was evident in every little glance they gave one another and the way Moulton could not look at her in the eyes for more than three seconds—like right now, in that moment, as they stood at the doorway of the shooting range.

"So look," Moulton said. "This may sound stupid and it might even be a little reckless, but I was wondering if you'd like to have dinner with me tonight. Like, not as partners."

Chloe was unable to keep the smile from jumping up on her face. She wanted to say something a little biting and sarcastic in response. Maybe a cliché *"Well, it's about time,"* or something like that.

Instead, she settled for a much safer and genuine: "Yeah, I think I'd really like that."

"If I'm being honest, I've wanted to ask you for a while now but…well, it was always so busy. And these last few weeks have been pretty much the opposite."

"I'm glad you finally decided to ask me."

That silence wrapped around them again and this time, he was able to meet her gaze without looking away. For a moment, she was pretty sure he was going to kiss her. But the moment passed and he nodded toward the doors.

"I'd better get to it," he said. "Call me later to let me know where you'd like to eat."

"I will."

She stood there for a moment, watching him enter the range. As far as the start of some sort of relationship, it had been awkward. It was the equivalent of a nervous pre-teen standing around at a dance when she'd heard that some cute boy had his eye on her. It made her feel incredibly naïve and juvenile, so she walked away as quickly as possible.

It was nearing five o'clock and since she had nothing on her schedule, she simply decided to head home. There was no use in going back to her little cubicle only to watch the last fifteen minutes or so tick away. Thinking of the time, she then realized that she didn't have much time to prepare for dinner with Moulton. She had no idea what time he preferred to have dinner but she assumed it would be sometime around seven—which gave her just a little more than two hours to figure out where to eat and what she was going to wear.

She hurried to the parking garage and got into her car. Here, she again fell into high-school-girl mode. What if they ended up in her car for some reason? It was pretty gross, considering she hadn't bothered cleaning it since she and Steven had split up. And as she thought of Steven, she realized *that* was why she felt so awkward easing her feet back into the dating pool. She had only had one serious relationship before Steven, and then she and Steven had dated for four years before getting engaged. She wasn't at all used to the dating scene and the idea of it seemed antiquated and, if she was being honest, a little scary.

She did her best to calm herself on her fifteen-minute commute to her apartment. She had no idea what Kyle Moulton's dating history was like. He could be just as out of the loop and rusty as she was. Of course, judging from his looks, she doubted this was the case. Honestly, if she was basing it all on just his looks, she had no idea why he was interested in her.

Maybe he's into girls with broken pasts and a tendency to throw themselves far too hard into their work, she thought. *Guys find that sexy these days, right?*

By the time she reached her street, her nerves had calmed quite a bit. The anxiety was slowly turning into excitement. It had been seven months since she had called it off with Steven. That was seven months without kissing a man, without having sex, without...

Let's not jump the gun, she told herself as she fit her car into a parking spot at the end of her block.

She got out of the car, mentally running through what she had in her closet that would look nice but not *too* nice. She had a few ideas of what to wear, as well as a few ideas of where they could go for dinner, as she had been craving Japanese as of late. Some sushi would really hit the spot, actually, and—

As she walked to her front stoop, she saw a man sitting on the top step. He looked rather bored, his head propped up in one hand while he scrolled through his phone with the other.

Chloe slowed a bit and then came a complete stop. She knew this man. But there was no way he could be here, sitting on the steps to her apartment building.

There's no way...

She took another slow step forward. The man finally noticed her and looked up. Their eyes met and when they did, Chloe felt her heart shudder.

The man on the steps was Aiden Fine—her father.

CHAPTER TWO

"Hey, Chloe."

He was trying to sound normal. He was trying to make it sound as if it were a perfectly normal thing to have him show up on her step. Never mind the fact that he had been in prison for nearly twenty-three years, serving time for playing a hand in the murder of her mother. Sure, recent events that she herself had uncovered showed that he was likely innocent of those charges, but to Chloe the man would always be guilty.

But at the same time, she had a small yearning to go to him. Maybe to even hug him. There was no denying that seeing him here, out in the open and free, stirred up a huge range of emotions within her.

She didn't dare move a step closer, though. She didn't trust him and, worse than that, she did not fully trust herself.

"What are you doing here?" she asked.

"Just wanted to come by and visit," he said, getting to his feet.

A million questions swirled through her head. Chief among them was how he had found out where she lived. But she knew that anyone with an internet connection and stubborn determination could figure that out. Instead, she tried to be civil without being warm and inviting.

"How long have you been out?" she asked.

"A week and a half. I had to work up the nerve to come see you."

She recalled the phone call she had made to Director Johnson when she had found that last piece of evidence two months ago—evidence that had apparently been more than enough to free her father. And now here he was. Because of her efforts. She wondered if he even knew what she had done for him.

"And this is exactly why I waited," he said. "This...this silence between us. It's awkward and unfair and..."

"Unfair? Dad, you've been in prison for most of my life...for a crime I now know you weren't guilty of but didn't seem to mind taking the fall for. Yes, it's going to be awkward. And given the reason for your incarceration and the last few conversations we've

7

had, I hope you understand if I don't come to you, dancing and tossing flowers your way."

"I absolutely get that. But...there's so much time we've missed. You might be unable to feel that yet, being so young. But those years I wasted in prison, knowing what I sacrificed...time with you and Danielle...my own life..."

"You sacrificed those things for Ruthanne Carwile," Chloe spat. "That was your choice."

"It was. And it's a regret I've had to live with for nearly twenty-five years."

"So what do you want?" she asked.

She moved toward him and then past him, toward her door. It took more willpower than she thought to pass by him, to be that close to him.

"I was hoping we could grab dinner."

"Just like that?"

"We have to start somewhere, Chloe."

"No, actually we don't." She opened her door and turned back to him, looking him in the eyes for the first time. Her stomach was in knots and she was doing everything she could not to get emotional in front of him. "I need you to leave. And please don't ever come back."

He looked genuinely hurt but his eyes never left hers. "Do you really mean that?"

She wanted to say yes, but what came out of her mouth was "I don't know."

"Let me know if you change your mind. I have a place in—"

"I don't want to know," she interrupted. "If I want to get in touch, I'll find you."

He gave her a thin smile, but there was still some pain there. "Ah, that's right. Working with the FBI now."

And what happened with you and Mom is what led me down that path, she thought.

"Bye, Dad," she said, and stepped through the door.

When it closed behind her, she did not bother looking back. Instead, she made it to the elevator as quickly as she could without appearing as if she were in a hurry. When the doors slid closed behind her and the elevator started going up, Chloe pressed her hands to her face and started to cry.

***

8

She stared into her closet, thinking very hard about calling Moulton and letting him know that she couldn't make it tonight after all. She wouldn't tell him the real reason why—that her father had gotten out of prison after spending twenty-three years there and had suddenly showed up on her doorstep. Certainly he'd understand the trauma of that, right?

But she decided that she was not going to let her father ruin her life. His shadow had hovered over far too much of her life already. And even something as small as canceling a date because of his presence was giving him too much power over her.

She called Moulton's number and when it went to voicemail, she left her suggestion for a dinner spot. With that done, she took a quick shower and got dressed. As she was slipping into a pair of pants, her cell phone rang. She saw Moulton's name on the display and her mind went to the worst scenarios first.

He's changed his mind. He's calling to cancel.

She actually believed this until the moment she answered the phone. "Hello?"

"So yeah, Japanese sounds good," Moulton said. "Now, maybe you can tell because of the extreme lack of detail and follow-through, but I don't do this much. So I don't know if I come pick you up or if we just meet there…?"

"Pick me up, if you don't mind," she said, again thinking of the ragged state of her car. "There's a pretty good place not too far from here."

"Sounds good," he said. "See you then."

…I don't do this much. Even though he'd admitted such a thing, Chloe still found it hard to believe.

She finished getting dressed, fussed with her hair a bit, and waited for a knock on the door.

Maybe it'll be your father again, she told herself. Although really, if she was being honest, it wasn't her own voice that was speaking to her. It was Danielle's voice, condescending and confident.

I wonder if she knows he's out yet, Chloe thought. *My God, she'll be absolutely furious.*

She didn't have time to dwell on this, though. Before she could, there was a knock at the door. For one paralyzing moment, she was sure it was her father. It made her freeze for a second, unwilling to answer it. But then she recalled how Moulton had been just as uncomfortable as she had been outside of the shooting range and she realized just how badly she wanted to see him—especially after the way the last few hours of her life had gone.

She answered the door, putting on her best smile. Moulton had one of his own. Maybe it was because they rarely saw one another outside of work, but Chloe found his smile sexy as hell. It also helped that while he had dressed rather plain—a button-down shirt and a pair of nice jeans—he looked incredibly handsome.

"Ready?" he said.

"Absolutely," she said.

She closed the door behind her and they headed out into the hallway. Once again, there was that perfectly still silence between them, one that made her wish they were a bit further along. Even something as simple and innocent as him reaching out to hold her hand...she needed something.

And it was that simple need for human contact that showed her just how much she had been rocked by her father showing up.

It's only going to get worse now that he's out of prison, she thought as she and Moulton took the elevator down to the lobby.

But she was not going to let him ruin this date.

She pushed all thoughts of her father out of her mind as she and Moulton stepped out into a warm evening. And to her surprise, it actually worked.

For a while.

CHAPTER THREE

The Japanese restaurant she had selected was a hibachi grill–type place, with the big open stovetops to allow large groups to sit around and watch the cooks perform their artistry. Chloe and Moulton opted for a table in the quiet, more private area of the restaurant. When they were both seated, she was pleased to find that it felt natural to be in a setting like this with him. Physical attraction aside, she had liked Moulton from the first moment she had met him. He had been the one shining light in a day where she had been switched from the Evidence Response Team to the Violent Crimes Program. And here he was, still making awkward moments in her life more bearable.

She didn't want to ruin the night with such conversation, but she also knew that if she didn't get it off her chest, it would be a needless distraction.

"So," Moulton said, picking at the corners of his menu as he opened it. "It wasn't odd that I asked you out?"

"I'm sure it depends on who you ask," she answered. "Director Johnson might not think it's the best idea. However, in keeping with honesty," she said, "I've kind of been hoping you'd ask."

"Ah, so you're a traditionalist? You wouldn't have asked me out? You would have waited for me to ask?"

"It's not so much being a traditionalist as it is being scarred from a past relationship. Which I supposed I may as well let you in on. Up until about seven months ago, I was engaged."

The shock on his face was only momentary. Fortunately, she saw no fear or awkwardness there. Before he could comment on this, the waitress came by to take their drink orders. They both ordered a Sapporo, placing the orders quickly, as not to let the momentum of their conversation stall out.

"Can I ask why it fell apart?" Moulton asked.

"It's a long story. The condensed version of it is that the guy was overbearing and couldn't separate himself from the shadow of his family—his mother in particular. And when I suddenly had a career with the FBI sitting right there in front of me, he wasn't very supportive. He also wasn't at all supportive of my own family issues…"

11

It then occurred to her that he probably knew about some of her family history. When she had gone digging it up near the end of her training, she was well aware that it had made the rounds of the academy grapevine.

"Yeah, I heard bits and pieces about that…"

He let the comment hang. Chloe took that to mean that if she wanted to tell him about it, he would listen. But if she'd rather not go there, he was fine with that, too. And at the moment, with everything that was on her mind, she figured it was now or never. *No sense in waiting,* she thought.

"While I'll spare you the details for some later day, I guess I should let you know that I saw my father today."

"So he's out now?"

"Yes. And I think it's mostly because of discoveries I made about my mother's death over the last several months."

It took Moulton a while to figure out where to go from there. He, too, used sipping from his beer as a method of taking his time. When he had a large gulp of it down, he replied with the best answer he could have.

"Are you okay?"

"I think so. It was just very unexpected."

"Chloe, we didn't have to go out tonight. I would have understood if you called it off."

"I almost did. But I didn't see the point in giving him control over yet another part of my life."

He nodded and they both took the silence that followed as a time to look over their menus. The silence remained between them until the same waitress came back to take their orders. When she was gone, Moulton leaned across the table a bit and asked: "Do you want to talk about it, or are we ignoring it?"

"You know, I think I'd rather just ignore it for now. Just be aware that there might be times tonight where I might be distracted."

He smiled and slowly got up from his chair. "That's fair. But let me try something, if that's okay."

"What?…"

He took a large step toward her, bent down a bit, and kissed her. She jerked back at first, unsure of what he was doing. But when she realized his intent, she let it happen. Not only that, but she kissed him back. It was soft but with just enough urgency to give her the idea that he had been thinking about this probably as long as she had.

He broke the kiss before it started to get uncomfortable; they were, after all, sitting in a restaurant surrounded by other people. And Chloe had never been one for public displays of affection.

"Not that I'm complaining," she said, "but what was that for?"

"Two things. It was me being brave…something I am rarely able to do with a woman. And it was also me giving you another distraction…hopefully one that can outweigh the distraction of your father."

With her head swimming a bit and warmth radiating through her entire body, she sighed. "Yeah, I think that might just have done it."

"Good," he said. "Also, I suppose it negates the whole *are we supposed to kiss at the end of this date* nonsense that I always screw up."

"Oh, after that one, we better," she said.

And, as Moulton had hoped, thoughts of her father's sudden appearance seemed very distant.

***

Dinner went much better than she could have hoped. Once they wrestled around the topic of her father showing up and then continued onward after Moulton's unexpected kiss, it went very smoothly. They talked about learning the ins and outs of the bureau, music, movies, acquaintances and stories from their time at the academy, their interests and hobbies. It felt natural in a way she had not been expecting.

Sadly, it made her wish she'd gotten rid of Steven sooner. If this was what she had missed out on by taking herself off of the dating scene for him, she had missed out on a lot.

They'd finished eating but stuck around for a few more drinks. It was another opportunity for Moulton to display his care and affection as he stopped at two drinks while Chloe had a third. He even asked if she'd feel more comfortable taking a cab if she was uncomfortable with him getting behind the wheel.

He took her back to her apartment, pulling up to the curb a little after ten o'clock. She was far from drunk but had a nice enough buzz going to wonder about things she might not otherwise entertain.

"I had a great time," Moulton said. "I'd like to do it again very soon if you don't think it will get in the way of work."

"Me, too. Thanks for finally asking me."

13

"Thanks for saying yes."

Never one to claim she was a master at the art of seduction, she responded to that comment by leaning in and kissing him. Like the kiss in the restaurant, it started slow but then started to build. His hand was suddenly on the side of her face, slipping down to the back of her neck to pull her closer. The armrest was between them and she found herself tilting her body to allow her hand to find his chest.

She wasn't sure how long the kiss went on. It was slow and wildly romantic. When they parted, Chloe found herself slightly out of breath.

"So, we've already covered the fact that I never really got to date," she said. "So if I do this next part wrong, you'll have to forgive me."

"What part?"

She hesitated a moment but the three drinks urged her on. "I want to invite you in. I'd make the claim that it's for coffee or another drink, but that would be a lie."

Moulton looked genuinely surprised. It was a look that made her wonder if he had misread her. "Are you sure?" he asked.

"That sounded bad," she said, embarrassed. "What I meant was…I'd like to do this without an armrest between us. But I'm not…I'm not going to sleep with you."

Even in the dim light, she could see his face redden at this comment. "I never would have expected you to."

She nodded, a little embarrassed herself. "So…do you want to come in?"

"I *really, really* do."

With that, he kissed her. This time, it was a bit more playful. In the midst of it, he elbowed the armrest in jest.

She broke away from him and opened her door. As they walked to the stoop of her building, she could not remember the last time she'd felt herself so…so *floaty*.

Floaty, she thought with a smile. It was a word Danielle had once used in explaining what it felt like to come down off of the physical high of an orgasm. The memory suddenly had Chloe feeling warm all over, reaching out and taking Moulton's hand as they entered the building.

They took the elevator and when the doors closed, Chloe surprised herself by pressing him against the elevator wall and kissing him. Now able to properly place her hands on him, she grabbed him by his waist and pulled him to her. This kiss was a bit

14

more passionate, hinting at so much more she wanted to do to him in that moment.

He was just as eager, his hands finding the small of her back. When he pressed her closer to him and their bodies met, she let out the tiniest of gasps. It was a little embarrassing.

The elevator came to a stop and she pulled away. She could only imagine the looks on the faces of the people she shared the building with if they caught her making out in an elevator. She was relieved to find that Moulton looked a little out of sorts and was breathing a little heavily.

She led him down the hallway, four doors down to her apartment. It then occurred to her that other than Danielle, Moulton would be the only person to have visited her apartment.

It's a shame I don't plan on wasting time with a tour, she thought.

It was yet another thought that made her feel a little embarrassed. She had never felt quite this physically needy when it came to a man. After a while, sex had become this formulaic, expected thing with Steven. And if she was being honest with herself, the times she had been left satisfied had been few and far between. And because of that, she hadn't really had much of a desire for any sort of intimacy with him.

Chloe unlocked the door and they stepped inside. She flipped on the kitchen light and hung her purse on one of the barstools.

"How long have you been here?" Moulton asked.

"Six months or so, I guess. I don't really have much company."

Moulton stepped to her and placed a hand at her waist. When they leaned in and kissed, it was slow and purposeful. It only took a few moments before he gently pressed her against the bar and their kiss deepened. Chloe felt herself growing breathless again, feeling a level of desire she had not felt since becoming intimate with a boy for the first time in high school.

She broke the kiss long enough to lead him to the couch, where they sat next to one another and immediately continued. It felt good to simply be with a man in such a way, especially one who made her feel like this. If she included the portion of her relationship with Steven where physical intimacy had practically gone cold, she had not been kissed and touched by a man like this in about a year and a half.

Eventually, after what felt like mere seconds but was in reality more like five minutes, she was leaning into him and he had no choice but to lie down. Chloe lay on top of him and when she did, one of his hands found its way up the back of her shirt. That small skin-on-skin touch pushed Chloe to an edge she did not see coming. She sighed against him and he responded by slipping his hand further up her back and running it along the side of her bra.

She sat up, straddling him, and smiled down at him. Her head felt like it was swimming and every muscle in her body was begging for more.

"I meant what I said," she said almost apologetically. "I can't sleep with you. Not so soon. I know it might seem old-fashioned…"

"Chloe, it's fine. You tell me when it's enough and we're good. Tell me when I've worn out my welcome."

She smiled down at him. The response was almost enough to make her change her mind. But she felt strongly that they should not be rushing this. Sitting on top of him on her couch was already pushing her limits.

"The welcome won't be worn out," she said. "Would I sound like too much of a headcase if I asked you to stay? No sex, but like…actually *sleeping* together?"

The offer seemed to surprise him. She supposed it *was* rather strange.

And do you know why you're asking such a thing? It was Danielle's voice in her head, always mocking but also helpful at the same time. *It's because Dad showed up today and screwed your world up. You want Moulton here so you won't be alone tonight.*

"I'm sorry," she said. "That seems conflicting and dumb and—"

"No, it's okay," Moulton said. "That sounds nice. I do have one thing to ask, though."

"What's that?"

"More kissing, please," he said with a smile.

She returned the smile and happily obliged.

***

She stirred awake some time later to Moulton getting off of the couch. She lifted herself up on one elbow. Her shirt had come off during their make-out session but that had been it. It had been weird to fall asleep on her couch with her pants on but she was oddly proud of their restraint. She glanced at the clock on the wall and saw that it was 5:10 in the morning.

"You okay?" she asked.

"Yeah," he said. "I just…I felt weird sleeping over. I didn't want it to be weird in the morning. I thought it might be best if I left. But at least there's not the added awkwardness of sex."

"Maybe that was my plan all along," she joked.

"Should I rush out and we pretend this didn't happen?" Moulton asked.

"I think I'd like you to stay. I'll put some coffee on."

"Yeah?"

"Yeah. I think I'd really like that, actually."

She slipped her shirt back on and made her way into the kitchen. She went about setting the coffee up while Moulton slid his own shirt back on.

"So it's Thursday," he said. "I don't know why, but it feels like Saturday."

"Is it because what we did last night is usually reserved for Friday nights? A way to kick off the weekend?"

"I don't know," he said. "I haven't done something like that for a while."

"Get out of here," she said as she set the coffee maker to brew.

"Seriously. Junior year of high school, I think. That was good year for me in terms of make-out sessions without the sex."

"Well, you apparently didn't miss a beat. Last night was…well, it was much more than I was expecting when you picked me up."

"Same here."

"But I'm glad it happened," she added quickly. "All of it."

"Good. Maybe we can do it again. This weekend, maybe?"

"Maybe," she said. "But my restraint is already feeling weakened."

"Maybe that was *my* plan after all," he said with a sultry smile.

She blushed and looked away quickly. She was a little taken aback by how much she enjoyed seeing him in such a flirty state.

"Look," she said. "I need to grab a shower. You're welcome to anything in the fridge if you want breakfast. There's not much there, though."

"Thanks," he said, seemingly unable to take his eyes away from her.

She left him in the kitchen and went into the bedroom, which the larger bathroom was connected to. She stripped down, turned on the water, and stepped into the shower. She almost felt like giggling over how the night had gone. It had made her feel like a teenager, enjoying the feeling of him there with her and feeling comfortable enough with him to know that he wasn't going to pester her for sex.

It had been romantic in an odd way and there had been two moments where she had nearly gone back on her claim of not sleeping with him. With a glee she was not used to, she secretly hoped he might decide to summon up the nerve to come join her under the water.

If he does, all restraint is going out the window, she thought.

She was just about done with her shower when she did indeed hear him enter the bathroom.

Better late than never, she thought. Her entire body tensed up with excitement and she found herself instantly eager for him to join her.

"Hey, Chloe?"

"Yes?" she asked, a bit provocatively.

"Your phone just rang. Maybe I was being nosy…but I looked. It was from the bureau line."

"Really? I wonder if something has come up…"

She then heard the ringing of another cell phone. This one was closer, presumably in Moulton's hand. Chloe peeked out of the shower, pulling the curtain slightly to the side. They exchanged a look before Moulton answered his phone.

"This is Moulton," he answered. He stepped back out of the bathroom and into her bedroom. Realizing why, Chloe turned off the water. She grabbed a towel from the rack and stepped out, grinning at him when he stared while she quickly wrapped the towel around her. Just because they had made out for about an hour and a half last night did not instantly mean she was okay with him seeing her completely naked.

There wasn't much of a conversation to eavesdrop on. It was mainly just Moulton listening and saying, "Okay…yes, sir…" a few times.

The call lasted about a minute and when he was done, he comically poked his head into the bathroom.

"Is it okay for me to come in?"

Wrapped in a towel that covered all of her private spots, she nodded. "Yes. Who was that?"

"That was Assistant Director Garcia. He said he tried to call you but you must have slept through it." He smiled at her and then went on. "He said I should call you or come by and wake you up. There's a case they want us on."

She chuckled as she stepped out of the bathroom and into the bedroom. "You think last night will affect the way we work together?"

"It might cause me to sneak into your motel room after hours. Other than that…I don't know. We'll see."

"Would you pour me a cup of coffee? I need to get dressed."

"I was sort of hoping I could use your shower."

"Of course. Though it would have been nicer if you'd asked ten minutes ago when I was still in there."

"I'll know better next time," he said.

As he went to the shower and Chloe started to get dressed, she realized that she was happy. *Quite* happy, in fact. Throwing a new case on top of all that had happened last night…it seemed as if her day had not been devastated by the sudden appearance of her father at all.

But if living with such an estranged family history had taught her anything, it was that you never truly escaped it. One way or the other, it always seemed to catch up with you.

CHAPTER FOUR

At roughly the same moment Chloe was being reminded what it felt like to lose herself in a man, her sister was in the middle of a nightmare.

Danielle Fine was dreaming about her mother again. It was a recurring dream she'd been having since the age of twelve or so—one that seemed to take on a different meaning with each stage of life Danielle entered into. The dream was always the same, never changing in detail or plot.

In the dream, her mother was chasing her down a long hallway. Only, it was the version of her mother that she and Chloe had discovered that day as young girls. Bleeding, wide-eyed, and lifeless. For some reason, the dream had always assumed she'd broken a leg in the fall (even though there were no official reports of any kind that had ever suggested such a thing) so the dream version of her mother dragged herself across the floor in pursuit of her daughter.

Despite the injury, her dead mother was always right on her heels, just a few fingertips away from grabbing her little ankle and pulling her down to the floor. Danielle ran away from the grisly vision in terror, her eyes cast to the end of the hallway. And there, standing in a doorway that seemed a universe away, was her father.

He would always be kneeling, opening his arms to her with a huge smile on his face. But there was blood dripping from his hands and in a moment of dream-panic that always woke her up, Danielle would stop running, stuck between her dead mother and her maniacal father, unsure of which direction was the safest.

It was no different now. The dream came to a crashing conclusion, jarring Danielle awake. She sat up in bed slowly, so accustomed to the dream now that she knew what it was even before she was fully awake. Groggily, she looked over to the clock and saw that it was only 11:30. She'd only been asleep for about an hour this time before the dream had come sneaking in.

She lay back down, knowing that it would take a while before she'd be able to go back to sleep. She shook the dream away, having learned many years ago how to shut it out by reminding herself that there was nothing she could have done to keep her mother from dying. Even if she had come clean with all of her little secrets about things she had seen and heard and experienced in regards to her father's toxic personality, there was nothing she could have said or done that would have kept her mother alive.

She turned over and looked toward the bedside table. She almost reached for the phone to call Chloe. It had been three weeks since they'd last spoken. It had been tense and awkward and it had been her fault. She knew she had been projecting a lot of negativity toward Chloe, primarily because Chloe didn't hate their father with the venom and angst that she did. It had been Danielle who had made the call three weeks ago, realizing that Chloe was waiting for her to make the next move since the last conversation they'd had before that had not gone so well—with Danielle practically telling her sister not to reach out.

But she didn't know Chloe's schedule. She had no idea if 11:30 was too late. Truth be told, Danielle had been having trouble falling asleep before two in the morning as of late. Tonight was one of her rare nights off from the lounge and also a night where she was not needed for any sort of sign-offs or approvals for the renovation of the bar her boyfriend bought for her.

She quickly pushed all thoughts of work out of her head as she searched for sleep. If she started thinking about work and everything on her plate, she would never get back to sleep.

Once again, she thought of Chloe. She wondered what sorts of dreams and nightmares her sister had about their parents. She wondered if she was still hung up on the idea of freeing their father and, if so, whether she had decided to keep it to herself.

Eventually, sleep caught back up to her. When it did, Danielle's last thought was of her sister. She thought of Chloe and wondered if it was finally time to forgive and forget—to let the memories of their father stop roadblocking her from a meaningful relationship with Chloe.

She was surprised at how happy the thought made her…so happy that when she did fall asleep again, there were the thinnest little traces of a smile on her face.

***

The young bartender who had been hired as her replacement had caught on quickly. She was twenty years old, drop-dead gorgeous, and was like some sort of savant at reading drunk men. Because she was doing so well, Danielle was able to meet with her boyfriend and the contractors at the building that would be her own pub and restaurant in about a month and a half.

Today, there was HVAC work being done, as well as some last-minute paneling in a back room that would serve as a reserved room for larger parties. When she arrived at the scene, her boyfriend was looking over a contract with an electrician. They were sitting at one of the tables that had recently been unpacked— one of three set-ups Danielle was supposed to choose from in terms of the types of tables she'd have in the restaurant.

Her boyfriend saw her as she entered. He quickly said something to the electrician and then came over to meet her. His name was Sam Dekker and while he wasn't necessarily the most honest or intelligent man, he made up for it in rugged good looks and a shrewd yet refined business acumen. He was about eight inches taller than she was so when he gave her a quick kiss, he had to lean down to do so.

"Reporting for duty," she said. "What can I do today?"

Sam shrugged, looking around the place in an almost theatrical fashion. "Honestly, I don't think there's too much you can do. It's all starting to fall into place. I know it might seem silly, but you might want to start looking through the ABC catalogue and figure out which brands of liquor you prefer to serve. Go ahead and figure out where you want the little overhead speakers for music and things like that. Those are the sorts of things that get lost in the shuffle and suddenly pop up as last-minute nuisances near the end of the project."

"I guess I can do that," she said, a little disappointed.

There were days when she stepped onto the renovation site and felt as if Sam was really just entertaining her—giving her menial tasks to do so he could handle the important things. It felt degrading in a sense but she also had to remind herself that Sam knew what he was doing. He had opened three bars that were doing incredibly well, one of which he sold to some big national company last year for more than ten million dollars.

And now he was choosing to back her in her own little endeavor. It was an endeavor that he'd had to talk her into. He insisted that she had the smarts to run a place like this, but only after all of the moving parts had been set into place.

Most girls that date semi-wealthy guys get jewelry and cars, she thought as she walked to the soon-to-be lounge area. *Me...I got a bar. Not a bad deal, I guess.*

She did feel a little out of her depth most of the time when she thought about the road ahead. She'd actually be in charge of a place. She'd be running things and making decisions. There was also a degree of guilt to it as well. She felt the opportunity had been handed to her for no real reason other than she had happened to end up in a relationship with a guy that knew how to get businesses started. As a result, she was aware that there were many things she had to sacrifice and things she simply allowed Sam to get away with. She never questioned his late nights out, always buying the stories that he was in meetings or with contractors, wining and dining them. She'd been a part of some of those meetings, so she knew it was true—most of the time.

She also felt that she had to show her appreciation as often as she could. That meant not nagging when she didn't see him for several days. It meant not getting too up in arms when he expected certain things in the bedroom. It meant not getting pissy because despite buying her a bar and trusting her to run it, the whole idea of marriage had not been mentioned a single time. Danielle was pretty sure Sam had no intentions of getting married. And for now, she was fine with that, so she saw no reason to argue about it.

Besides…what did she have to complain about? She'd finally met a guy who treated her like royalty—when he was around—and she seemed to be on a path to easily earned success.

It's because most things that seem too good to be true usually are, she thought.

When she reached the room that was going to be the lounge area, she pulled the digital blueprints up on her phone. She made indications where the speakers could go and also made a note about potentially adding some sort of tinted window along the back wall. It was in doing things like this that she felt the dream of it all becoming a reality. Somehow, this was all really happening to her.

"Hey…"

She turned and saw Sam standing in the framed doorway. He was smiling at her and looking at her with the hungry expression he often shot her way when he was feeling frisky.

"Hey yourself," she said.

"I know it seems like I just brushed you off," he said. "But really…these next few weeks, all I'm really going to need from you are a few signatures."

"You're working me too hard," she joked.

"I fully intended for your training with the newbie at the bar to take longer. It's not my fault we ended up hiring a bartending

23

genius." He approached her and wrapped his arms around her waist. She had to look up into his eyes but it always made her feel safe for some odd reason; it made her feel like this man would always *literally* watch over her.

"Let's grab lunch later today," Sam said. "Something simple. Pizza and beer."

"Sounds good."

"And tomorrow…what do you say we go somewhere. A beach…South Carolina or somewhere like that."

"Really? That seems spontaneous and very much like a burden to all of this work around us. In other words…it sounds nothing like you."

"I know. But I've been getting so wrapped up in this project and…I realize I've been neglecting you. So I want to make it up to you."

"Sam, you're giving me my own business. That's more than enough."

"Fine. I'll be selfish about it then. I want to get away from all of this and be naked and alone with you near the ocean. That sound better?"

"It does, actually."

"Good. So go to the bar, check in on the newbie. I'll pick you up for lunch around noon."

She kissed him and although he was clearly rushing it, the sentiment of everything he had just said did not escape her. She knew it was hard for him to be emotional and sincere. She rarely saw that side of him so when she did, she dared not question it.

Danielle walked back through the mostly open spaces of the old brick building that would soon be her bar-slash-lounge. It was hard to think of it as hers, but that was very much the case.

When she stepped outside, the sun seemed brighter than it had when she had gone in. She smiled, still trying to make sense of everything her life had become. She thought of Chloe again and made the decision to call her in the next few days. Everything else in her life was going so well, she may as well try repairing the tense relationship between her and Chloe, too.

She got into her car and headed back to Sam's other bar—the bar he had hired her to work in six months ago. She was so distracted by the thought of going away with him for the weekend that she didn't notice the car parked on the side of the street as it inched out into traffic behind her.

If she *had* noticed it, she might have recognized the driver, though she hadn't seen him in a very long time.

Still, did a daughter ever truly forget what the face of her father looked like?

CHAPTER FIVE

When Chloe and Moulton arrived at Garcia's office, Director Johnson was already there, waiting for them. It appeared that he and Garcia had been looking through case files; Garcia had a few pulled up on his desktop screen while Johnson had a small pile of printouts in front of him.

"Thanks for coming so quickly," Johnson said. "We've got a case out in Virginia—a small town on the other side of Fredericksburg, in an upscale neighborhood. And I should probably start with saying that the victim's family has some very powerful political friends. That's why we've been called in. Well, that and the gruesome nature of the death."

As Chloe took a seat at the small table in the back of Garcia's office, she did her best not to seem too obvious that she was trying to create some distance between herself and Moulton. She knew that she was probably glowing, beaming from the way the night and the morning had gone. She wasn't sure how Johnson might react to any kind of relationship between them and she honestly didn't want to test it.

"What are we looking at?" Chloe asked.

"Four days ago, a husband came home from work to find his wife dead," Garcia said. "But it was more than that. She had not only been murdered, but brutally so. There were multiple stab wounds—sixteen by the coroner's count. The crime scene was a mess…blood everywhere. It's unlike anything the local PD has ever seen."

He slid a folder over to Chloe with a look of warning on his face. Chloe took it and opened it slowly. She peered inside, saw just a flash of the crime scene photo, and then closed it just as quickly. Based on her one glimpse alone, it looked more like a slaughterhouse than a murder scene.

"Who is the victim's family friends with?" Moulton asked. "You said someone in politics, right?"

"I'd really rather not give out that information," Johnson said. "We don't want it to seem as if the bureau plays favorites when it comes to bipartisan matters."

"What's the level of local police involvement?" Chloe asked.

"They've kicked off a county-wide manhunt and have the State PD involved," Garcia said. "But they're being asked to keep it quiet. The local PD is understandably upset because they feel like we're hindering a case that is already a bit outside of their comfort zone. So I need you to get down there as soon as you possibly can. Also...and please listen closely: I thought of you two for this case because of how well you've worked together in the past. And Agent Fine, you seem to have a knack for this small-town, isolated community sort of crime. However, if the case itself and those crime scene photos make you feel uneasy—like it might be a little too much for you to handle at this stage of your career—let me know now. I won't judge and it won't count as any sort of mark against you."

Chloe and Moulton exchanged a look and she could see that he was just as eager as she was to take the case. Still, unable to help himself, Moulton took a look at what was inside the folder. He grimaced a bit as he flipped past the few crime scene photos and scanned the very brief report in the back. He then looked back over to Chloe and gave a nod.

"We're good as far as I'm concerned," Chloe said.

"Same here," Moulton said. "And I appreciate the opportunity."

"Glad to hear it," Johnson said, getting to his feet. "I'm excited to see what you two can do. Now...get moving. You've got some driving to do."

***

Moulton was behind the wheel of the bureau car, heading off of the beltway and heading toward Virginia. Barnes Point was only an hour and twenty minutes away, but the Beltway made just about *anywhere* feel like it was on the other side of the planet.

"You sure about this?" he asked.

"About which part?"

"Working together on a case like this. I mean...we were making out like two horny teenagers about ten hours ago. Will you be able to keep your hands off of me while we're working?"

"Don't take this the wrong way," Chloe said, "but after what I saw in that folder, doing that with you again is the farthest thing from my mind."

Moulton nodded his understanding. He veered off onto the next ramp, hit a straight stretch, and stepped on the gas. "All jokes aside, though…I enjoyed last night. Even before the part back at your place. And I'd like to do it again. But with work…"

"We should remain strictly professional," she finished for him.

"Exactly. And, to that end," he said, sliding his iPad out of the hollowed center of the console, "I downloaded the case files while you were packing."

"Did you *not* pack?"

"You saw my bag. Yes, I packed. But I'm quick about it." He shot her a cute little sly grin as he said this, indicating that she had perhaps taken a bit longer than he had expected. "I didn't get a chance to look it over, though."

"Ah, some light reading material," Chloe said.

They both chuckled and when Moulton rested his hand on her knee while she started to read the file, Chloe wasn't sure they *would* be able to keep it professional.

She perused the case files, reading the important parts out loud for Moulton. They found that Garcia and Johnson had done a fine job of summing it up. The police report was quite detailed, as well as the pictures. They were still no easier to look at and Chloe didn't blame the local PD. She figured *any* small-town police force might be out of their element on something this violent and bloody.

They shared thoughts and theories and by the time they passed a sign telling them that Barnes Point was fifteen miles away, Chloe had changed her mind. She thought they *would* be capable of working professionally together. She had spent the last few weeks so wrapped up in her physical attraction to him that she had nearly forgotten how sharp and intuitive he could be when it came to casework.

The idea then occurred to her that if they could truly make this work, she might have what just about every woman on the planet desired: a man who respected her as an equal in career and intellect but also in the bedroom.

You're not even a day into this, a voice said in her head. Danielle's voice again. *Are you really getting all dreamy and ga-ga about it already? Jesus, you made out with him for a few hours and didn't even sleep together. You barely know him and—*

But Chloe chose to shut those thoughts away.

She then turned her attention to the coroner's report. It told the same story Johnson had told them, but in more detail. And it was these details that she focused on. The blood, the violence, the potential political motive. She read them over, studying with intense focus.

28

"I'm thinking this isn't politically motivated," she said. "I don't think the killer was too concerned with the powerful political friends that the Hilyards might have had."

"I heard confidence in that statement," Moulton said. "Please explain."

"Lauren Hilyard was stabbed sixteen times. And every single wound was centered in the abdomen area, with only a single stray one slicing into her left breast. The coroner reports that the wounds were ragged and almost on top of one another, indicating someone made stabbing motions one right behind the other. The note here in the reports says: *as if in a blind rage or frenzy.* If this was the act of someone with political motivation, there would likely be some sort of message or other indicator."

"Okay, then," Moulton said. "I'm on board. It's not politically motivated."

"That was easy."

He shrugged and said, "I'm coming to understand that people in DC think *everything* has political motivations. So what if the Hilyards maybe sort of kind of know someone higher up in a political office. Not everyone is going to care."

"I like the way you think," she said. "But I don't know that we rule it out one hundred percent just yet."

They were closing in on Barnes Point, and the fact that they had been entrusted to round up a case with potential political ties was not lost on her. It was an amazing opportunity for both of them and she had to make sure that was where her focus was for the time being. For now, nothing was more important than that—not suddenly reappearing estranged fathers, not the voice of her stubborn and joy-dead sister...not even a potentially perfect romance with the man sitting next to her.

For now, there was the case and only the case. And that was more than enough for her.

CHAPTER SIX

Barnes Point was a quiet yet cute city, with a population right at nine thousand. The Hilyard residence sat just outside the city limits, in a little subdivision called Farmington Acres. The victim's husband, Jerry Hilyard, had not yet been able to bring himself to return to his home since discovering his wife's body; with no immediate family living nearby, he had been invited to say elsewhere in the neighborhood, with close friends.

"I think I might have needed to get farther away than just a few houses down," Moulton said. "I mean, can you imagine what this poor guy is going through?"

"But he might also need to be close to his home," Chloe suggested. "To the place where he and his wife had shared a life together."

Moulton seemed to consider this as he drove their rental car further into the subdivision, toward the address the State Police had forwarded them while they'd been en route. It was yet another example of how Chloe was beginning to both understand and respect the fluidity of the way the bureau worked. It was hard to imagine that just about any information she needed—addresses, phone numbers, work histories, criminal records—was readily available, just a call or email away. She assumed agents eventually got used to this, but for now, she still felt quite privileged to be part of such a system.

They arrived at the address and walked to the door. The mailbox read *Lovingston* and the house itself was a carbon copy of just about all of the other homes in the neighborhood. It was the sort of neighborhood where the houses were right on top of one another but the environment was quiet—a good place for kids to learn to ride their bikes and probably a lot of fun during Halloween and Christmas.

Chloe knocked on the door and it was answered right away by a woman with a baby in her arms.

"Are you Mrs. Lovingston?" Chloe asked.

"I am. And you must be the FBI agents. We got a call from the police a while ago saying you'd be on your way."

"Is Jerry Hilyard still staying here?" Moulton asked.

A man appeared behind the woman, coming from the open room to the left. "Yeah, I'm still here," he said. He joined Mrs. Lovingston at the door and leaned against the door frame. He looked absolutely exhausted, apparently not having slept well ever since he had lost his wife in such a brutal fashion.

Mrs. Lovingston turned to him and gave him a glare that made Chloe think the baby in her arms might be in for some nasty looks in the future. "You sure you're up to this?" the woman asked him.

"I'm fine, Claire," he said. "Thanks."

She nodded, held her baby tighter to her chest, and headed back elsewhere in the house.

"Come on in, I guess," Jerry said.

He led them into the same room he had come in from. It looked to be a small den of sorts, mostly decorated with books and two elegant-looking chairs. Jerry fell into one of the chairs as if his bones were starting to give out on him.

"I know Claire might seem a little hesitant about you being here," Jerry said. "But...she and Lauren were good friends. She thinks I need to be grieving...which I am. It's just..."

He stopped here and Chloe could see him wrestling with a flood of emotion, trying to make it through this conversation without crumbling in front of them.

"Mr. Hilyard, I'm Agent Fine and this is my partner, Agent Moulton. I was wondering if you might be able to tell us about any political ties your family might have."

"Jesus," he breathed. "It's overblown. The local PD made a huge fuss about it and got all freaked out. I'm pretty sure that's why you were called in, right?"

"*Are* there political ties?" Moulton asked, sidestepping the question.

"Lauren's father used to be really good golf buddies with the Secretary of Defense. They grew up together, played football together, all that. They still hang out on occasion—duck hunting, fishing, things like that."

"Did Lauren ever speak with the Secretary?" Chloe asked.

"Not since we've been married. He came to our wedding. We get a Christmas card from his family. But that's about it."

"So do you think what happened might be due to that relationship?" Moulton asked.

"If it is, I have no idea why. Lauren was not into politics at all. I think it's just her father's way of making himself seem important.

Someone killed his little girl so it *must* be because he knows important people. He's kind of an ass like that."

"So what can you tell us about the last few days of Lauren's life?" Chloe asked.

"I've already told the police everything I could."

"We understand that," Moulton said. "And we have copies of all of their reports. But for us to properly get a foothold here, we may be asking you some questions that have you repeating a few things."

"Fine, that's good," Jerry said.

Chloe thought the man might not quite be aware of what was happening, exactly. He looked incredibly detached. If she didn't already know the traumatic situation he was going through, she might have assumed he was on drugs.

"The first question may seem silly in light of what has happened," Chloe said, "but can you think of anyone who might have had a reason to be upset with your wife?"

He sneered and shook his head. When he spoke, his voice trembled in a sort of eternal yawn. "No. Lauren stayed to herself these days. An introvert. It had gotten even worse as of late…drawing into herself, you know?"

"Any idea why?"

"She had a rough past. Messed up parents and all that. She was sort of a bully in high school. I guess that's what she'd be classified as these days. Or maybe a mean girl. She'd been coming to terms with those mistakes as of late. I think it got worse when she got that damned high school reunion invitation in the mail."

"She was anxious about going?" Chloe asked.

"I'm not sure. It made her sad, I think…to think about the people she had maybe been mean to."

"Did the two of you graduate together?" Moulton asked.

"We did."

"And did you go with her to the reunion?"

"God no. I hate that sort of stuff. Posturing and pretending to like people you mostly hated in high school. No. I sat it out."

"You say she was an introvert," Chloe said. "Did she not have many friends?"

"Oh, she had a few. Claire was one of them. And the friends she did have were like family to her. They were extremely close."

"Have you spoken with them since this happened?" Moulton asked.

"Just one. She called shortly after she found out to see if I needed anything."

"Are these friends that perhaps went to the reunion with her?"

"Yeah. Claire went, too. But she's also sort of an introvert. I think she went just out of curiosity."

"Do you and Lauren have any children?" Chloe asked. "A neighborhood like this, I figured there would be at least one kid in every house."

"We have two. Our oldest, Victoria, is eighteen; she just started college this year. She...well, she chose to spend this very difficult time with her grandparents. And because she went with them, our youngest—Carter—wanted to go, too. I've never had the best relationship with my in-laws but my kids being with them right now is a godsend. I feel like a terrible father, but if my kids were here, I'd crumple up and just break, I think."

"Is there any animosity about your children being with their grandparents right now?" Moulton asked.

"I want them here with me...just to see them. But I'm a mess. And until the house is in better shape...that's where they need to be."

"You said your oldest *chose* to be with them during this time," Moulton said. "Why is that?"

"She couldn't wait to get out of our house. She had a strained relationship with Lauren for the last few years. Some toxic mother-daughter stuff. Our daughter...she was having boys over, sneaking in the house at night. She was doing this as young as thirteen. Had her first pregnancy scare at fifteen. And if you do the math in your head...Lauren was thirty-seven. We had our daughter when Lauren and I were both nineteen."

Chloe thought the tumultuous family situation could not be making this any easier on Jerry Hilyard. She didn't think there was anything there worth digging into, though it might do some good to eventually speak with the daughter.

"Mr. Hilyard, would you have any objection to us taking a look around your house?" she asked.

"That's fine. The sheriff and a few of his men have been in and out a few times. The code to get in is two-two-two-eight."

"Thank you, Mr. Hilyard," Moulton said. "Please contact us if you think of anything else. For now, I think we'll speak with Mrs. Lovingston to see if she has any details to share."

"She's told the police everything she knows. She's starting to get irritated, I think."

33

"What about her husband? Did he know your wife well? Did the four of you frequently hang out together?"

"No. Claire's husband works out of town quite a bit. I did FaceTime him to make sure he was okay with me staying here. And anyway, it was mainly just Claire and Lauren. They had a weekly thing where they'd drink wine on the front porch, switching houses every week."

Claire stepped into the room slowly, apparently having put the baby she had been carrying down for a nap.

"And we'd do the predictable things that women do. Talk about our husbands, reminisce about the past. I'd tell her about the highs and lows of having a baby. And, more recently, we'd talk about what she was going through with her daughter."

"What can you tell us about Lauren and what might have led someone to do such a thing to her?" Chloe asked.

"Lauren made some decisions during high school that her parents did not particularly agree about," Claire replied. "Once Lauren graduated high school and had her daughter...well, college was out of the picture."

"They were embarrassed," Jerry added. "They got pissed and moved to New Hampshire. They feed our daughter these brutal lies about Lauren whenever they can."

"Trying to make up for the mistakes and neglect from raising Lauren," Claire said. "A couple of real assholes."

Sensing the conversation headed to a bashing session, Chloe spoke up. "Mrs. Lovingston, would *you* happen to be able to think of any enemies or even strained relationships Lauren might have had?" Chloe asked.

"Not outside of her family. And while they are a couple of jerks, they certainly wouldn't do this. This is...this is deplorable."

Moulton reached into his inner pocket and pulled out a business card. He placed it on the coffee table and stepped back. "Please...if either of you think of anything else, please don't hesitate to contact us."

Both Claire and Jerry gave only curt nods. The conversation had been brief but it had taken its toll on them. Chloe and Moulton made their exit in an awkward silence.

When they were outside, heading for the car, Chloe paused for a moment on the sidewalk. She looked down the street, in the direction of the Hilyard house, and saw that it was just out of sight. Still, she was starting to agree with Moulton. Maybe it was a little too close. And if the bedroom still looked anything like what she had seen in the photographs Johnson had showed them, it seemed almost morbid that Jerry was staying so close.

"Ready to go check out the house?" Chloe asked.

"Not really," Moulton said, the images he'd seen from that case file still clearly in his mind. "But I guess we've got to start somewhere."

They got back into the car and headed back the way they had come. Right away, Chloe kept telling herself that it couldn't be as bad as it had appeared in the pictures—all of that crimson red among the crisp white sheets.

***

It took all of twenty seconds to get to the Hilyard house. The fact that it closely resembled the Lovingston house—and most every other house on the block—was creepy as hell as far as Chloe was concerned. They entered through the front door with the code Jerry Hilyard had given them and stepped into an absolutely still and silent house.

Knowing exactly why they were there, they wasted no time and went directly upstairs. The master bedroom was easy to find, the room all the way at the end of the hallway. Through the opened door, Chloe could already see streaks of red on the carpet and the sheets.

She was relieved, however, to find that the scene truly didn't look as bad as it had appeared in the pictures Director Johnson had showed them. First and foremost, the body had been removed. Secondly, the bloodstains had been sitting longer, making them paler in color.

They walked to the bed, careful to step over any blood splashes left on the carpet. She could see areas in the blood splatter where the coroner and initial investigators had accidentally stepped in it. Chloe looked to the other side of the room, toward a dresser and where a small flat-screen TV was mounted to the wall. *She was probably watching TV when it happened, maybe purging her head of high school reunion memories…*

Chloe then went downstairs and had a look around. She could see no signs of forced entry and no clear indications that anything had been stolen. She looked around the living room, the kitchen, and the guest bedroom. She evens stepped out on the back deck and had a look around. There was a small patio table in the corner. An ashtray sat in the center of it, under the shade umbrella.

Chloe made a *hmm* sound as she saw the ashtray's contents. There were no cigarette butts in the tray, but some other kind of ash and paper. She leaned down to it and took a light whiff. The scent of marijuana was unmistakable. She sorted through some things in her head, trying to figure out if this could be relevant in any way.

Chloe jumped a bit when her phone rang. Moulton, stepping out onto the back porch to join her, caught her look of momentary shock and smiled. She rolled her eyes and answered the call, not recognizing the number.

"This is Agent Fine," she answered.

"This is Claire Lovingston. I thought you might want to know that I just got a call from one of my friends, Tabby North. She was one of the close friends that Jerry was telling you about. She asked if anyone else from the police had come to speak with me. I told them the FBI had just visited and she'd like to speak with you."

"Does she have information for us?"

"Honestly…I don't know. Probably not. But this is a rather small community. I think they just want to get to the bottom of it. I'm sure you'll find them incredibly helpful."

"Great. Text me her number after this call."

Chloe killed the call and filled Moulton in. "That was Claire. She said one of Lauren's other friends called her to see if anything new had developed. She'd like to speak with us."

"Good. I won't lie…I'm pretty much done here. That bedroom is giving me the creeps."

It was a good way to explain it. Chloe could still see the pictures in her head, so seeing the scene without the body was like looking into some old abandoned place she was not meant to see.

Still, they went back to the bedroom and took some time to check the place over, looking in the bathroom, the walk-in closet, even under the bed. After finding nothing of interest, they left the house and, moments later, the Farmington Acres neighborhood. Chloe again thought that it was incredibly quaint—a perfect neighborhood to grow a family and shape a future.

So long as you were okay knowing that, from time to time, there might be a murder to contend with.

CHAPTER SEVEN

Tabby North was a redhead who had the kind of body that Chloe assumed saw the gym at least four days a week; it was also a body that, in Chloe's humble opinion, could use a few more meals. She was gorgeous in a very obvious way, but she looked as if a strong wind might blow her away.

Chloe and Moulton met Tabby at her house and found that she had invited another close friend, a woman who apparently went to that very same gym with Tabby. This woman was Kaitlin St. John, who was crying when Chloe and Moulton showed up. They gathered together on Tabby's screened-in back porch, where Tabby treated them to a pitcher of lavender lemonade. Chloe could not help the thoughts that blew through her head—of how pretentious it all seemed, these women quickly approaching forty, with their tiny waists and trendy health-nut drinks.

These thoughts are certainly not why Johnson stated he thought you had a knack for these small neighborhood-based cases, she thought to herself.

To be polite, she sipped from the lemonade. Despite her negative thoughts, it was actually delicious.

"I assume you ladies have already spoken to the police?" Chloe asked.

"Yes," Tabby said. "And while I fully understand that they are doing their best, it was quite clear that they had no idea what they were doing."

"They're spooked, too," Kaitlin said.

"Spooked by what?" Moulton asked.

"By the idea that it might have some sort of political reasoning. I guess you know about Lauren's dad being all buddy-buddy with the Secretary of Defense. I'm sure the local police would rather avoid a media circus if they can help it."

"So, *is it* politically connected?" Tabby asked.

"It's far too early to know for sure," Chloe said. Already, she was getting an uncomfortable vibe from these two. She did not doubt their grief; it was apparent in their expressions and the fact that Kaitlin had been openly crying since they'd showed up. But she also had no real problem picturing these two sitting around—

perhaps with Lauren Hilyard and Claire Lovingston—gossiping about everyone in town. She wondered how much of what they might discuss right here and now would end up hitting the Barnes Point grapevine.

"Can you tell us when you last saw Lauren?" Moulton asked.

"It was the night before she died," Tabby said. "We all met up at our high school reunion."

"We practically had to drag Lauren to it," Kaitlin said. "She always hated that kind of thing."

"Well, she hated that sort of thing *after* school was over," Tabby corrected. "She always wanted to try to leave the high school years in the past."

"Did she seem any different that night?" Chloe asked.

"Nothing that I noticed," Tabby said.

"Same here," Kaitlin said. "I daresay she ended up having some fun later on in the night. Lauren…well, she was the heartthrob of our high school. All the guys wanted her and when Jerry Hilyard just happened to knock her up during senior year…man, it was like the place had exploded. She lost some of that allure, you know. But the way everyone treated her that night at the reunion…I think everyone forgot about that. And it was like she was the queen bee all over again. I think she needed that."

"Was there a big crowd?" Moulton asked.

"Pretty big," Tabby said. "This is sort of a strange part of town. Lots of people that went to our high school either graduated or ended up coming back this way after college. It's not exactly a wealthy city, but this side of town is known for being the wealthy side, you know? Anyway, for a few moments, Lauren actually looked happy."

"We understand that Lauren was among those that graduated and stayed around," Chloe said. "Were you all friends in high school?"

"Yes. Hell…Lauren and Claire were friends from kindergarten."

"So would you say they were the closest out of the four of you?"

"Probably," Kaitlin said. "They've always been besties. We know they had their little private porch sessions. It's sweet…but yeah, from time to time, I felt a little left out. How about you, Tab?"

Tabby shrugged. "Not really. I always knew they were super close."

"Was there anyone at the reunion that maybe crossed Lauren the wrong way?" Moulton asked.

"Not that I remember," Tabby said.

"Same here," Kaitlin said. "But you know…you live in a place like this where a lot of the people you grew up with stick around for the long haul and things can get tense sometimes. It was obvious between *some* people at the reunion. But not with Lauren. I don't think she really had many people that disliked her in high school. Jealous for sure…but not *dislike*."

"Did you maybe meet up with anyone else at the reunion that Lauren was friendly with in high school but sort of drifted away from afterwards?"

"We did, actually," Tabby said. "A woman named Brandie Scott. She lives in town, too. Just on the other side…so we never really see her. It was nice to reunite with her, though. I wouldn't say we were all that friendly with her, just maybe talked to her a few times in school, but never hung out."

"Did she and Lauren hang out at the reunion?"

"For a while. I actually specifically remember them laughing about something over by the bar. I remember because Lauren hadn't really laughed a lot recently. I think she had something going on at home. Maybe with her stupid parents again."

"Would you happen to have Ms. Scott's phone number?" Moulton asked.

"I do," Tabby said, taking out her phone and starting to scroll. "I actually got it from her the night of the reunion."

"What about ex-boyfriends?" Chloe asked as Tabby found the number. "Were there any of Lauren's exes in attendance?"

"No," Kaitlin said, smiling for the first time during the conversation. "Lauren only ever dated one guy before Jerry. And the only reason they broke up was because he moved. To Alabama, I think."

"Well, I think that's all we need for now," Chloe said. She slid Tabby one of her business cards and said: "Please send Ms. Scott's information to this number. And don't hesitate to contact me if either of you think of anything else that may be helpful."

Tabby texted Brandie Scott's number right away. She looked a little disappointed that the conversation was over. But, as Chloe had suspected from the start, a group of best friends that were caught up in memories of the friend they had just lost was not going to be the best source of information. If there was any dirt to uncover, she and Moulton were not going to find it here.

She took one last sip from her lemonade and got to her feet. Both of the women escorted them back through the lovely house and through the front door. They both stood on the porch and watched as Chloe and Moulton left.

"Initial thoughts?" Moulton asked.

"I think they're both very sad about the loss of their friend," Chloe said. "But I also think that just about every word of the conversation we just had with them will be public knowledge in Barnes Point by the end of the day."

"I got that same feeling, too. And tell me…maybe it's just me. Is there something sort of weird about these older women hanging out in the same city, in the same circles they were in during high school?"

"I for one would never do it," Chloe said. "But I don't think it's as uncommon as you might think. Especially in smaller towns."

Moulton started the car and pulled away from Tabby North's house. "Want to check out this other sort-of friend?" he asked. "Brandie something-or-another?"

"Already on it," she said, saving the number Tabby had sent her to her contacts list. She then placed the call, already hoping that the woman on the other end would turn out to be at least somewhat different from the thin and almost cliché housewives she'd met so far today.

***

As Tabby had said, Brandie Scott lived on the other side of Barnes Point. It was only a fifteen-minute drive between the houses, but Brandie Scott may as well have been living on the other side of the world. Where the carbon copy two-story homes in the expensive plots within Farmington Acres and surrounding areas painted a picture of wealth and well-to-do homeowners, the other side of town was quite different. There were mobile home parks and one-story homes that looked nearly abandoned, many with sings that either read FOR SALE or CONDEMNED on them. There were old shops that had been closed for quite some time. This side of town looked like something the better part of town had perhaps vomited up and tried to cover up hastily in its tracks.

Brandie Scott had agreed to meet them at a little coffee shop on a street that showed some of the signs of neglect as the rest of the area but was still somehow alive and thriving. When Chloe and

40

Moulton entered the place, all eyes were on them—which weren't many, seeing as how it was 4:15 on a Thursday afternoon.

A slightly overweight woman waved to them from the third table to the right. She did so as quickly and subtly as she could, as to not draw more attention to herself. Chloe and Moulton walked over to her and the woman visibly grew tense.

"Brandie Scott?" Moulton asked.

"That's me," she said. "Have a seat, I guess."

The agents did so and once they were seated, Brandie seemed to relax her posture just a bit. "I hate to be a nag," she said, "but I don't have much time. I had to ask for an hour off of work to come here to meet you."

"Oh, I'm sorry," Chloe said. "You work here in town?"

"I do. I have two jobs, actually. I work nights as a janitor out at the hospital in Farmville. And I also squeeze in about twenty hours a week at Dollar General here in town…which is what I'm doing now."

"You sound like a busy lady," Chloe said. "We'll make it as quick as possible. We assume you know about what happened to Lauren Hilyard?"

"Yeah, I heard. Tabby North told me two days ago."

"Since it happened, have you spoken to the police?"

"No. They haven't reached out."

"Well, as I told you on the phone, we just came from Tabby North's house where we spoke with her and Kaitlin St. John. They mentioned that you and Lauren weren't ever particularly close, but that you talked quite a bit at the high school reunion over the weekend."

"Yeah, we did. They're right…Lauren and I were never really close. But unlike a lot of those women, Lauren at least made a point to try to be polite when she saw me."

"What do you mean by *those women*?" Moulton asked.

"Women like Tabby North. Claire Lovingston and that whole bunch. Some of them think the rules of high school still apply—that they're required to continue to oust the girls that weren't popular in school."

"But you say Lauren wasn't like that?" Chloe asked.

"It depends on who you ask. If I'm being honest, she was one of those mean girls in high school, you know? She was never really mean to me but went out of her way to ignore me. I'd like to think that changed with her after high school…but I don't know her well enough to be sure. The few times I ran into her, she seemed a little different…not quite as mean-spirited."

"Do you recall her having a lot of enemies in high school?"

"There were plenty of people that were jealous of her. But I think hate might be a strong word. People like me, if I'm being honest, were very jealous of her. She was beautiful and had the attention of all of the guys. But it was mostly jealousy, you know? She was that unattainable girl…the girl all the dudes wanted and all the girls wanted to be. You know the type? So while there were plenty of people that surely didn't like her, I think it would be a stretch to call those people enemies."

"So when you spoke with her at the reunion, was it cordial or sort of forced?" Chloe asked.

"It was a very friendly conversation. She had come into Dollar General a few days before to get some sort of weed killer for her flower beds. We chatted a bit then and when I saw her at the reunion, I was just being polite—asked her how her flowers were doing. It got us on a tangent about some stupid project we'd had to do for biology in high school."

"Even though she was polite to you on occasion after high school, do you know if there were any people she was *not* polite to?"

"Oh, I'm sure there are several. One person that instantly comes to mind is the woman that used to work as a nanny for the Hilyards."

"What's the story there?"

"Well, years ago, Lauren was working as a hairdresser in the better part of town. And Jerry had the same job he has now—some sort of marketing or copywriting job for the only ad firm here in Barnes Point. So there were a lot of late hours. This was years ago, when Victoria still needed a babysitter and wasn't old enough to watch Carter herself. They hired a nanny and from the way the story goes, it didn't last very long. Some sort of altercation took place between Lauren and the nanny. There are about a hundred versions of the story floating around town but the way I understand it, Lauren ended up slapping this woman and pushing her off of the front porch, screaming at her. There was some talk of the nanny pressing charges but it never came to anything."

"If that story is true, does it jive with how you remember Lauren in high school?" Moulton asked.

"Maybe not to that extreme, but yes…it reminded me a lot of the Lauren I knew back then. *If* the whole story is true."

"Can you think of any other stories like that since after graduation?" Chloe asked.

Brandie thought about it for a moment and then shook her head. "No. That's the only one that sticks out."

"Do you happen to have a name for that nanny?" she asked.

"Yvonne Dixon. She's still here in town. Lives right up the street in one of the Gladstone Apartments, in fact."

"Are you close with her?" Chloe asked.

"No. But on this side of town, you tend to start to know where everyone lives. I'm pretty sure she'd be open to talking to you. And I don't know what it is...but it always seems that babysitters and nannies always have the best gossip. The most truthful gossip...if there's such a thing."

During the course of her brief career, Chloe knew that this did tend to be the case. She assumed it was especially true in a smaller community like this. Having a nanny who once worked for the Hilyards as a potential lead made the case feel like it had some wheels to it—like they might wrap this thing before barely even got started.

CHAPTER EIGHT

Chloe did her best to keep her feelings in check, but being an active agent was still so new to her that it made her want to break out into a grin whenever she had the chance to flash her ID and badge. She found herself doing just that as she and Moulton spoke with the owner/landlord of the Gladstone Apartments complex.

"FBI?" the owner asked, genuinely shocked. "What on earth do you need to speak with Ms. Dixon for?" He was an aging man, pushing sixty, hiding his stark white hair beneath a John Deere hat.

"We're not at liberty to say," Chloe said. "Although, for your peace of mind, I can assure you it's not in regards to anything she's done."

"It's about that Lauren Hilyard murder, isn't it?" the owner asked.

"I'm sorry sir, we really can't say," Moulton echoed.

"Can we please just get her apartment number and contact information?" Chloe asked.

The owner nodded and went to a tattered filing cabinet behind his desk. He flipped through a few papers and brought one back over to them. It had her apartment number listed, as well as her phone number and last known residence before becoming a resident of Gladstone Apartments.

Chloe snapped a picture of the document with her phone and nodded her thanks to the owner.

"Do you know if she's currently working anywhere?" Chloe asked.

"Working as a babysitter for some family out on the other side of town in one of those subdivisions."

"Farmington Acres?" Moulton asked.

"Nah, some other one. I don't know the names of all of them. But if you're looking to talk to her, I'm pretty sure she's home. I saw her car out there in the parking lot when I came back inside from cleaning out the gutters about half an hour ago."

"Thank you very much," Chloe said.

She and Moulton stepped back outside, Chloe looking to the picture she had snapped. "Apartment number seven," she said.

The apartment complex was two stories, each story holding eight apartments. It was the type of apartment building where the stairs were all outside and the entire place looked like one big house rather than an apartment building. They followed the order of the numbers on the door and found number seven at the very bottom corner of the first floor.

Moulton knocked on the door and they heard an immediate, "One second," called out from inside.

Yvonne Dixon answered the door about twenty seconds later. She was sweating a bit and the apartment behind her smelled like Lysol or Mop and Glo, or some similar cleaning product. She gave them a skeptical look, not opening the door all the way.

"Can I help you?"

Again, Chloe was delighted to flash her badge and ID. "We were hoping you might have some time to speak with us about your history with Lauren Hilyard."

Yvonne frowned slightly as she glanced back and forth between the agents. "I heard about that," she said. "It's...well, it's sad."

"We understand you used to work for her," Chloe said.

"Yeah, I did." She paused a moment, apparently seeing where this trail was going to eventually lead. She opened her door up and waved them inside. "Come on in. But excuse the mess. You caught me in the middle of cleaning."

They walked inside and Chloe found that while the apartment itself was small and rather dingy, Yvonne kept it tidy and clean.

"The landlord told us that you have a job out on the other side of town," Moulton said. "Did you have the day off?"

"No. I work for the Nelson family. The father is usually on the road, traveling for business. The mother works a dispatch position for the sheriff's department in town. She has some odd hours, usually forcing me to wake up around four in the morning. But it gives me the afternoons off; she's usually off of work by three or so."

"How long have you worked for this family?" Chloe asked.

"A little over three years."

"Well, according to the story around town, things didn't particularly end well with you and Lauren Hilyard."

"That's putting it mildly," Yvonne said. "I'm sure there are many versions of the story floating around town, but here's what *really* happened. Carter, their son, was five at the time. He was preschool age and Lauren had me going through this really simple and quick tutorial sort of thing to help prepare him for kindergarten. She much preferred that over sending him to one of the preschools in town. The kid was bright as all get out and whenever he did exceptionally well, I'd give him a Blow Pop as a reward—a reward, mind you, that Lauren approved of.

"Well, this one day…I still don't know how it happened, but Carter got the gum from the Blow Pop in his hair. And he didn't bother telling me. He was playing in his room then comes down and tells me it's been there for like fifteen minutes. I did my best to get it out with some weird methods I found online—dish soap, peanut butter, all that. But nothing worked. I tried calling Lauren but she never answered her phone. So I made a judgment call and I cut it out. It didn't *butcher* his hair or anything, but it was noticeable. When Lauren got home and saw it, she went right the hell off. She had lost her temper with me several times before, but this was *bad*. This was nuclear."

"We heard she slapped you," Moulton said.

"Yeah, she did. She asked me to step out on the porch to talk. I assumed it was so her kids wouldn't hear us arguing. The moment I stepped out there, she started screaming at me. The moment I tried to get a word in, she slapped me. Busted my lip and took me by such surprise that I damn near fell down her porch steps."

"I assume she fired you that day?" Chloe asked.

"That's just the thing. When I didn't show up the following day, she called to see where I was…like she fully expected me to come in. It was like she was pretending nothing had happened. She eventually apologized for slapping me. But of course, I never went back to work for her."

"Did you speak to her at all after that? Like maybe whenever you might have happened to pass by one another in town?"

"No. It was always just dead silence. Jerry did try to approach me one day in the grocery store to make amends but I told him I wasn't interested."

"Do you remember what she was like in high school?" Moulton asked.

"I didn't go to school around here. I moved to Barnes Point for a guy. A guy that ended up beating on me and moving away. But then I was sort of stuck…"

"How are you typically treated by the little groups of women around town?" Chloe asked. "I know this place can be a bit clique-y."

"I'm never *mis*treated, but it's clear that if you haven't *always* been part of the group, you aren't welcome in."

"So it's safe to say that you have an unbiased opinion of the friend groups around here?"

"I suppose so. I will say that most of the women around here come off as being stuck up. Like they're better than you. Which is dumb. Because if they were all that, why the hell did they stick around a place like Barnes Point after high school or college?"

"Well, given your rather neutral position on the town and its people," Chloe said, "can you tell us of anyone else you think might have been rubbed the wrong way by Lauren Hilyard?"

"As a matter of fact, yes. Just last week, I heard that she had fired the guy they had coming in to rework her flower beds."

"Did things get out of hand?" Moulton asked.

"From the way I hear it, it did. A little screaming match and everything. It wasn't until later that I found out the guy she had hired was sort of a creep. And I think that's why Lauren fired him."

"What do you mean?"

"The guy is a Hispanic dude that doesn't live around here, but used to do a lot of work for the wealthier families. A jack-of-all-trades sort of guy. Landscaping, light carpentry, that sort of thing. Then word got out that he got caught peeking into windows and...um, well, pleasuring himself while he peeked."

"Do you have a name for this guy?"

"Sorry, no. But he drives a blue truck with one of those ladder and utility racks on the back. The sticker on the side of the truck says First Choice Handyman."

"How reliable would you say this story is?" Chloe asked.

"Pretty reliable. I heard it from a woman that lives a few houses down from the Hilyards. She works at the bank and those ladies are *always* gossiping. She said she and her husband were out for a walk when Lauren had her little shouting match with him."

"Thank you very much for your time," Chloe said.

"Sure," Yvonne said. "But...there are people talking. Saying that Lauren's death is related to some sort of political stuff. Is that true?"

"It's really just too early to say," Chloe said. "But hopefully the information you just gave us can help us find out."

Yvonne seemed pleased with this, giving them the faintest of smiles as they walked toward the door. She opened it for them and saw them out, giving them a wave as they got into the car.

"First Choice Handyman," Moulton said as he typed it into his phone. He found the number on Google and called it right away.

"Let's find out if he was doing anything more that working the flower beds when he was at the Hilyards' residence."

CHAPTER NINE

When calling First Choice Handyman, Moulton was met with a voice message. The recorded message told him that business hours were from eight to five and that if he left a message, someone would call him back soon. Moulton did not leave a message. Instead, he went back to the Google search results and found out more about the business. It was owned by a man named Oscar Alvarez. The business had several reviews on Google and Yelp. The ones that specifically mentioned the man's level of work were all great. But many of them seemed to be bemoaning the fact that he had been caught masturbating while looking through windows. One even suggested that Oscar Alverez peddled child pornography.

"Damn, the internet can be a mean place," he said. "I wonder how soon we can get this guy's records from the bureau."

"I think we'd be better off just heading to the local police department to see what they have."

"And that's why you're considered the lead on this case," Moulton said with a smile.

They located the Barnes Point police station thirteen minutes later. It was located at the end of a rather long Main Street stretch that seemed to be situated right in the zone that separated the wealthier side of town from the other side of the tracks.

When they walked inside, the woman at the reception desk gave them a smile. Chloe wondered if Ms. Nelson—the mother of the family that Yvonne Dixon currently worked for—had been sitting there earlier in the day.

"Can I help you?" the woman asked.

"We're the FBI agents that were sent out to look into Lauren Hilyard's murder," Chloe said. "We were hoping to get some information about a man that we believe might be a suspect."

"Oh, you'll want to speak with Sheriff Jenkins," she said. "And boy, will he be glad to speak with you. I'll buzz him and let him know you're here. But go ahead and go on back. He's the last door on the left at the end of the hall."

They walked beyond the counter and through a door that the receptionist buzzed them through. They found the sheriff's office at the end of the hall, the door already open.

"Sheriff Jenkins?" Chloe asked.

The middle-aged man behind the desk looked up from a stack of papers he had been sorting through. Behind him, a map of the state was on the wall, marked up and labeled with various Post-its.

"Yeah?" he asked. But he seemed to understand who they were within another second or two…perhaps by the way they were dressed. "You with the bureau?"

"We are," Chloe said. They both showed their identification and introduced themselves. At once, Jenkins seemed relieved.

"Well, I don't have much on the Hilyard case," he said. "But what I do have, you're welcome to."

"We actually think we might have a lead," Chloe said. "We were wondering what you might be able to tell us about a guy named Oscar Alverez."

"Ah hell," Jenkins said, reclining back in his chair, looking as if it was the first bit of rest he had gotten all day. "How'd his name come up?"

"We spoke with a few people and discovered that Lauren Hilyard fired Alvarez last week, the day before the high school reunion."

Jenkins shook his head slowly. "See…I hadn't heard that yet. I've talked with everyone I could think of that was close to that family and didn't hear that a single time. I didn't even know they had hired Alvarez for anything."

"From what we gathered, he was leveling out the ground for the flower beds. There was apparently some huge fight, seen by one of the Hilyards' neighbors and then passed around the town grapevine."

"Well, *that* I can believe." He rolled his chair over to a filing cabinet and thumbed through some of the documents. Chloe wasn't sure why, but she always felt a certain charm whenever she watched someone use a filing cabinet. It was something reliable, something tangible and not encoded on some network or electronic filing system.

"Oscar Alvarez," Jenkins said, pulling out a folder and sliding it over to them. Moulton picked the folder up but didn't look through it yet. He seemed to be perfectly happy listening to Jenkins as he gave a play-by-play. "He was arrested for lewd conduct two years ago while building a back porch for the Harper family. According to Mrs. Harper, she saw him fondling himself one time but figured maybe he was…well, *adjusting* or scratching. But then she caught him trying to peer through her bedroom window while she was changing, again fondling himself. Forgive me for being so

50

crude, but he left some…*evidence* behind, right there on the side of the house."

"Did he do time for that?"

"Three days here in the cell and a three-thousand-dollar fine. He stayed away from Barnes Point for a while after that. He came in here about eight months ago, spoke to me directly, and swore that he was a changed man. Said he wanted me to be the first to know because he was going to try to drum up more business here in Barnes Point. I told him good luck because no one would hire him again based on what everyone knew of him. To my surprise, a few did hire him. Small stuff, mostly. He's cheaper than the well-known handymen and construction companies around here and, if I'm being honest, he does much better work."

"Where does he live?" Moulton asked.

"The town of Winston, about ten miles south of here. Lives in a double-wide off the road a bit."

"Has there been any more trouble with him?"

"No. Nothing serious. Sure, stories still circulate, but there's nothing to them. As far as I was concerned, he was true to his word: he was a different, improved man."

"You said as far as you *were* concerned?" Chloe asked.

"Yeah. I decided to look around…do some digging on him when he came back. It seemed like nothing serious at first. I'm not one to judge a man, you know? We all make mistakes."

After hearing this, Moulton opened the folder. There were only three sheets inside of it. He scanned them and read the juicer parts out loud. "Assault in 2003, spousal abuse in 2006, arrested for public indecency in Roanoke in 2009." Moulton raised his eyebrows. "And you never suspected a thing after he came to you?"

"I did, of course," Jenkins said, a little offended. And for a while, I continuously checked up on him. Drove by the job sites, called the people that hired him. And I never got a single complaint. However…the timing with his being fired by Hilyard and then her showing up murdered…yeah, that's hard to look past."

"Do you have an address for him?" Chloe asked.

"It's there in the folder. You want me to come along?"

"I don't think so. For now, let's just play it safe and pay him a visit…see what comes from it. But be ready to move in the event we need assistance. And if you have a cell or interrogation room, can you make sure it's ready to go?"

"Oh yeah, I can handle that."

Moulton was already typing Alvarez's address into his GPS app. When he had it plugged in, he nodded to Chloe. "Thanks, Sheriff," he said.

Chloe nodded to him as she exited the office. She saw that the aging sheriff looked a little relieved not to be headed out. She wondered if it was so he could place the blame solely on the FBI if this murder did indeed have ties to something political.

Best not to give him anything to place blame about, then, Chloe thought as they headed back through the station and out toward the car where night had started to fall.

***

The town of Winston made the lesser part of Barnes Point look classy by comparison. The little town consisted of a convenience store that doubled as a fried chicken restaurant and a post office. Anything else the town might have was hiding down the winding back roads that snaked into the rural Virginia woodland.

Because of the town's small size, they were able to find Oscar Alverez's address quickly. His double-wide trailer sat about a quarter of a mile off the road, visible only because of the rather well-maintained driveway. When they parked behind the truck that read First Choice Handyman on the side, Chloe noted the shed that was being built on the backside of the property. She recalled Jenkins saying the work Alverez did was better than anyone else in Barnes Point. If the foundation for shed was any indication, he was exactly right.

As they walked across the yard toward the porch, the porch light came on and the front door opened. A Hispanic man looked out at them, his dark hair and beard seeming to stretch out into the night.

"Who's there?" he asked.

Quick to come to the door when he saw headlights, Chloe thought. *Seems a little suspicious to me...*

She noticed Moulton stepping up ahead of her, taking a protective position. She couldn't help but smile as he slowly pulled his ID from his jacket pocket. "Agents Moulton and Fine, FBI," he said.

"FBI? What the hell for?"

His accent was not very thick. He sounded just like any other suspicious American. It made Chloe wonder just how long Alvarez had been in the country. She also wondered—perhaps a bit stereotypically—if he'd have anything to worry about in terms of legal standing as a US citizen.

"We'd just like to ask you some questions," Moulton said.

"No," Alvarez said, clear panic in his voice. "I've done nothing wrong."

"No one is saying you have," Chloe said. They had reached the porch by then but stopped at the bottom of the stairs. They wanted to give Alverez every indication that they were not here to be intrusive. "We're only here to ask about a woman you recently worked for."

Alvarez considered this for a minute and then stepped out onto the porch. He closed the door behind him and leaned a hip against the porch railing.

"Are you not going to invite us in?" Chloe asked.

"No. What woman are you talking about?"

"Lauren Hilyard. We were told you were working on flower beds for her and she fired you."

"Yeah, that lady is crazy. *Loco.*"

"Can you tell us why she fired you?" Moulton asked.

"I don't even know why, man. She said I was getting too much dirt in her yard. Said I was being too rough with the grass. And then she called me a pervert because of things I did in the past. That bitch started screaming at me, right in the front yard."

"Did you leave right away?"

Alvarez nodded, but stayed quiet.

"Yes or no, Mr. Alvarez?"

"I don't know what else you want to know. I left when she told me I was fired. She didn't even pay me. And I haven't bothered trying to get it out of her because I don't want to deal with her crazy ass again."

"Would it surprise you to know that Lauren Hilyard was killed several days ago?" Chloe asked.

She looked for some sign of shock on Alvarez's face, but there was none. If there had been, it would have been quite visible in the glow of the porch light.

"No, I did not know that."

"It's believed she was killed just a day or two after she fired you."

"Oh, and you think I did it?"

"I said no such thing," Chloe said. "You just happen to be the last person that she was in a verbal confrontation with."

"That makes me guilty?"

"Stop doing this," Moulton asked. "Look…you're refusing to allow us inside your house. You're being a little difficult with our questions. All of that *does* make you suspicious. Especially when you consider the criminal record you have."

"That's in the past. And I'm done with this. Goodnight, Agents."

"No, we aren't done," Chloe said. "Mr. Alvarez, can you give us proof of your whereabouts Saturday night and Sunday of last week?"

He nodded and said, "I could."

And then he opened his door and headed back inside.

"Mr. Alvarez, if I have to, I *will* arrest you. We can question you here or at the station."

"This is discrimination," Alvarez said. He gave a slight smile, as if he knew exactly what he was doing. "Prejudice."

"No, this is you being difficult to work with," Chloe said.

"And this," Moulton said, stepping up onto the porch, "is me arresting you."

He moved with a speed Chloe had not been expecting. It was almost like a dance in a way. He managed to spin Alvarez around and bring each arm behind his back without being too rough. By the time the cuffs were on Alvarez, he looked as if he wasn't quite sure what had just happened.

"Go," Moulton said. "To the car. *Now*, Mr. Alvarez."

The smile was no longer on Alvarez's face. He had tried to play the prejudice card and it had backfired. Besides…Chloe figured that this was not the kind of community that was going to toss him too much sympathy just because of his ethnicity. He had a criminal record and most of the people in Barnes Point already had negative views of him.

Guilty or not, she doubted anyone was going to have much sympathy for him in Barnes Point. She figured they'd find out soon enough as they escorted him in cuffs to the back of their car. He didn't say a word the entire time and came along easily enough. It made Chloe feel uneasy—a feeling that had still not let up by the time they reached the precinct.

CHAPTER TEN

Chloe and Moulton both sat on the opposite side of the small table, facing Oscar Alvarez. "I'm not exactly sure why you chose to do things this way," Chloe said. "If you are innocent, why not answer our questions?"

"Because I am tired of everyone doubting me. I am tired of everyone thinking that I did not change. I did very dumb things. But that was in the past. That is not me anymore."

"So where were you all day Sunday? That was when Lauren Hilyard was murdered. Can you give your whereabouts?"

"I was at home. Listening to the preacher from Lynchburg on my TV. After that, I went out for a while."

"Where?"

"To the grocery store. Then to a friend's house."

"Who is the friend?"

Alvarez shook his head. "They are not involved."

"We're not saying they are. But if we can get a picture of where you were around the time Mrs. Hilyard was killed, we can let you go. It's rather silly we had to bring you in the way we did."

"I agree," Alvarez said. "Am I being charged with her murder? Do you have evidence?"

"No, not at this time," Moulton said.

"So you will let me go. I know the laws."

Something occurred to Chloe, something that had gnawed at her a bit while they had been standing out on Alvarez's porch steps. "Excuse me for a moment," she said, mostly to Moulton, but loud enough so they could both hear her.

She stepped out of the small interrogation room. The viewing room was the next door down. She found Sheriff Jenkins there with two other officers, watching the interrogation on a small flat-screen television.

"I think we need to get someone over to Oscar Alverez's house," she said. "He's hiding something. And he was adamant about not letting us into his trailer."

"I'd need a warrant for that," Jenkins said.

"Go over and just check the place out. Don't go inside or anything like that. Take a look around. See if you can find some sort of justification for going inside."

"You think he's the killer?" one of the officers asked.

"No idea. But he *is* hiding something. And I think whatever it is will answer your questions."

"Let's hop to it then," Jenkins said. "You good here?" he asked Chloe.

"Yes. And thanks for your help."

As Jenkins and the officers left the room, Chloe walked back into the interrogation room. Moulton was in the middle of asking Alvarez if he'd had any shouting matches with other clients.

"I've had disagreements in the past, but nothing like that."

"Were you aware that a woman on the other side of the street, just a few houses down, saw the altercation?"

"No. I didn't know that."

Chloe took a breath and leaned forward, doing her best to appear sympathetic. "Level with us, Mr. Alvarez. We know you're trying to hide something—maybe some secret. And when we have you here trying to get answers in the midst of a murder investigation, that looks incredibly bad."

"No, I'm hiding nothing." But even as he said it, he looked away and stirred uncomfortably in his seat.

"The sooner you can tell us, the easier it will be on you. If you try to ride this out and we find out that you were lying…it's going to be bad. Even if whatever secret you have has nothing to do with Lauren Hilyard."

Alvarez looked to the table, to his interlaced fingers. He looked back at Chloe and Moulton, and then back to his hands—back and forth like a metronome as he wrestled with something.

"If I tell…there could be trouble. For me, maybe. But it's not me I am worried about."

"If you're honest with us, perhaps we can help," Chloe said.

He then chose to look at them directly. Chloe was shocked to see the glistening of tears in the corners of his eyes. "It is…my cousin."

"What about him?" Moulton asked.

"He is staying with me for right now. He hopes to find carpentry work somewhere. I wish I could hire him, but I can't. I am letting him stay with me until we find work for him somewhere."

"Why would you keep that a secret?" Chloe asked. But before the question was fully out of her mouth, she thought she knew. As an American, you couldn't turn on the news these days without hearing some story about it—no matter what side of the argument you fell on.

"How long has he been with you?" Moulton asked.

"Two days. I spent Saturday driving to Georgia to pick him up. We stayed overnight and came home Sunday. He came in somewhere by Eagle Pass, Texas, several days ago and has been hitchhiking ever since. He is not supposed to be here, according to the government. Please...he can't go back. Let me keep him here, for a better life."

Well, what a little mess we've stumbled into, Chloe thought.

"Is he at your trailer right now?" Moulton asked. "Is that why you would not let us come in?"

"Yes," Alvarez said.

"But he can confirm that you were on the road, coming back from Georgia, on Sunday?" Chloe asked.

"Yes, he can."

"And he's here illegally?" Moulton asked.

Alvarez nodded curtly and said: "Yes, whatever the hell that means."

"We honestly care nothing about that," Chloe said. "How that is handled will come down to Sheriff Jenkins. We are more concerned with the murder case. And if your cousin can clear you, then you are free to go."

She stood up again and mouthed *"One second"* to Moulton. She then stepped outside of the room and called Jenkins to give him a heads-up of what he was about to step into. She found herself legitimately concerned for Alvarez and the outcome of his situation—particularly while living in a rural town in the South.

Jenkins answered and Chloe filled him in. When she was done, she was met with a heavy silence that was broken only by Jenkins uttering a curse. He thanked her and then hung up, leaving Chloe to listen to a dead line.

CHAPTER ELEVEN

Danielle had gotten a lot accomplished in the past twelve hours but she still felt as if she had done no real work. She'd gone back to the bar and made sure the new bartender was still as good as always (she was) and then spent most of the rest of the afternoon talking to ABC vendors and audio installation experts.

Now she was relaxing at home—home being Sam's huge apartment—with a glass of wine and a book. It was 9:30, a full hour and a half after Sam was scheduled to be back home. It was nothing new, as he came and went all the time, his schedule keeping him consistently busy.

But as the clock ticked to 9:31, Danielle's suspicion grew too heavy to ignore. She walked to the bedroom and found his secondary iPad charging on the bedside table. She unlocked it (the code was the score of the Patriots vs. Falcons Super Bowl) and opened up his calendar. Under today's date, he had nothing scheduled for after 7 p.m.

She then went to his text messages. Her suspicion arose again when she found that there were only two text threads on it: one between him and her that went back several months, and another between him and the lumber provider he was using for the new bar and lounge remodel. But she had seen the countless text threads on his phone. Why had this iPad been cleaned out?

Stop pretending like you know anything about how technology works, she told herself. *Maybe most of the other messages go directly to his phone. What the hell are you looking for anyway?*

She set the iPad down and went back into the living room. No sooner had she picked up her glass of wine than she heard the familiar sound of his key in the lock. She quickly sat back down, wanting to assume the position of a woman who had lazily been lounging around, waiting for him to get home.

He came through the door carrying his briefcase in one hand and his more rugged and beaten up bookbag over his shoulder. There were also little flakes of sawdust in his hair. She sometimes made fun of the different roles he had to assume in the course of a day: one minute a bartender, the next, a carpenter; after that, a businessman.

"I know, I know," he said. "I'm late."

"And you have sawdust in your hair," she pointed out.

"Yeah, I know. I was playing with the skill saw down at the lounge. But hey…the stage is coming along great. Did you get those speakers we were talking about?"

"I did. They ship out tomorrow."

He set his bags down by the door and looked apologetically at her. "I know it's late. Did you have anything planned?"

"No. It's okay. We can do dinner or something tomorrow."

"You sure?"

"Sam…it's fine."

"Okay. Well…why don't you find something for us to watch? This sawdust is itching my neck and scalp. I need to hop in the shower."

"Yes, please do."

He stuck his tongue out at her and dashed from the kitchen to the large master bedroom. She listened to him rummaging around for a moment as she considered sneaking up on him in the shower. While the sex between them was still amazing, it had waned a bit as he had gotten heavily involved in the lounge project—*her* lounge project. It had been a little over a week; not only did she want it, but he'd appreciate a little spontaneous shower sex.

She got to her feet and tiptoed to the bedroom door. As she waited to be sure he was in the shower, a thought occurred to her, an itching doubt like an insect buzzing around her head.

"I was playing with the skill saw down at the lounge…the stage is coming along great."

This was a lie. She knew that the last of the cuts for the stage had been done yesterday. She'd called the contractor early this morning to make sure she had the right measurements for the speakers. But why would he lie about that?

She heard the closet in the bathroom open as Sam got a clean towel. Danielle dipped into the bedroom and stealthily made her way to the bathroom door just as Sam turned the shower heads on. He paused for a moment and walked back toward the mirror over the sink. Danielle ducked backward, nearly getting caught.

She watched from around the door frame as he looked at himself in the mirror. He was looking at something between his neck and shoulder. He sighed and said, "Damn."

The mirror was along the side wall, so she was able to spy on him without showing up in the mirrors. It also gave her a clear view of what he was so interested in on his neck.

Slight bite marks. A small and light bruise in the perfect shape of a mouth.

A hickey.

And I haven't kissed him like that in over a week, she thought.

Her anger got the better of her, flashing across her mind before any form of reason even had a chance. She stepped into the bathroom just as he backed away from the mirror.

"Something wrong?" she asked.

He wheeled around, clearly caught in guilt. But he tried to play it off as a cool sort of surprise. "Jeez, you scared the hell out of me!"

"Did the hickey come from the skill saw, too?" she asked.

"It's not a hickey," he said, though he subtly started to shift his head so that the area wasn't as obvious. "I think one of the boards I was carrying today must have rubbed me on the shoulder—"

"You're good at lots of things, Sam. But lying isn't one of them."

She then watched something take place within his expression that alarmed her. In the space of about two seconds, his countenance changed from concern to indifference.

"Really?" he asked, stepping toward her. It was only then that she realized he was completely naked, as he had been just about to step into the shower. "Because I've been doing it for about a month now and you're only now finding out."

"Who is it?" she asked. She wanted to cry, but she was just too mad.

"You don't know her. And it's none of your business."

"You're a bastard," she said. She turned away from him and stormed into the bedroom.

"We can talk about it when I'm out of the shower," he said.

"Going to get her smell off of you?" she screamed.

"Oh, shut up. What do you care, anyway? I'm giving you a life you would have never had if you hadn't met me. So don't even pretend like you're too good for this."

"For *this*?" she asked. "For what?"

"A man that gets some on the side."

"Go to hell," she said. "Take your shower. I'll be gone by the time you get out."

Sam laughed at this. He walked to the bedroom door, seemingly unaware that he was still nude or simply not caring. "That's hilarious. You're going to leave me?"

"I've left better men for much less," she said.

"Oh, I'm sure you have," he said, storming into the room. And then, as if he were doing nothing more casual than swatting at a fly, he reached out and slapped her. It hit hard, spinning her in a half circle, nearly making her go to the ground.

"I know about your past," he said. "Don't think I don't know how much you used to get around. I saved your sorry ass. And you're really going to leave me?"

The anger came flaring up again and she went barreling at him, throwing a wild left-handed blow. Had she been more focused and not so consumed with hatred, it might have done some real damage. Instead, it bounced off of his right arm. He responded in kind, slapping her again. The right side of her face felt like it had exploded. When she stumbled backward, he kept coming at her. He used both hands to shove her hard against the wall. The back of her head struck it and for a moment, she saw little black stars in her line of sight.

"You can't leave me, you silly little girl," he said. "Where will you go? What will you do? You've got a huge opportunity lined up for you. A business that could make you incredibly wealthy. And you're going to leave it because I like to get a stray piece every now and then?"

"Shut up," she said, afraid she might cry in front of him.

He came to her and pressed her against the wall in a way that was somewhere between threatening and sexual.

"You're not stupid," he said, leaning in and gently biting her lip just hard enough to hurt. "You aren't going anywhere."

She screamed in his face and he jolted a bit, smiling at her. It was exactly what she wanted. In his distraction, she brought her knee up hard and fast. Since he had no pants or boxers on, she was able to feel the connection and knew her aim had been dead on. He howled and dropped to the ground. He reached out for her leg but she was already out the bedroom door.

As he hurled insult after insult her way, calling her names she'd already heard many times before from many different men, Danielle ran straight for the front door. As she did, she was fully aware that she was not only running out on Sam, but on a bright future—a future that was right there in front of her, dangling like a poisoned carrot.

CHAPTER TWELVE

Chloe's phone rang just as she stepped into the main office of Barnes Point Motel 6. When she saw Danielle's name on the caller ID, she was conflicted. Conversations with Danielle had not exactly gone the best as of late. But as it was currently coming up on 10:30 at night, she followed her instincts. Danielle calling this late was probably going to result in bad news of some kind or another.

"I need to take this," she told Moulton as they approached the desk. "Can you handle getting the rooms?"

"Plural?" he asked, a playfully disappointed smile on his face.

She returned it and said: "Well, Johnson will get suspicious if there is only one room listed on the expense report. As for how you and I handle that later…I'll let you choose."

She stepped back out into the parking lot and answered Danielle's call. "Hey, Danielle. What's up?"

She heard a muffled sniffle followed by what sounded like a contained sob. Danielle was crying. It didn't happen often but when it did, it never failed to break Chloe's heart.

"I didn't know who else to call…" Danielle finally managed.

"Is everything okay? Danielle…what is it? What's wrong?"

"Sam…he hit me. Hard. Pushed me. He was cheating on me…and I…"

"Are you hurt?" Chloe asked.

"No…I. Ah Jesus, give me a second."

Chloe did just that. She listened as Danielle took several moments to get herself together. Heavy breaths, stifled sobs, and finally, a strained and tired voice finally speaking. "He faked putting sawdust in his hair and said he needed a shower. He had a hickey. Not from me. He put the sawdust in his hair just to have an excuse…to wash the smell of another woman off of him."

"And he hit you?"

"Twice. And then slammed me into the wall. I had to leave. I had to. I did the right thing, right?"

"Of course you did. Danielle…you should file a report. That's abuse."

"No. I don't want it dragged out."

"Where are you right now?" Chloe asked.

"My apartment. About twelve miles away from his place."

"Will he come for you?"

There was silence for a moment as Danielle thought about this. "Shit, I don't know. I don't know…Chloe, this is a mess."

"It'll be okay. Do you have some place else to go?"

"It's all gone," Danielle said. "The business he was building for me. The bright future, the escape from this miserable life…it's all gone." She sounded more angry than hurt now. In terms of Danielle, that was probably a good thing.

"Danielle, listen to me. Do you have anywhere to go?"

"I can just say here."

"Don't take that chance. He might come for you…and if you aren't going to call the police on him, that could be dangerous. You need to get out of there."

"And go where, Chloe? I have nowhere to go."

"Do you remember where my apartment is?"

"I can't stay with you," Danielle said, nervously laughing off the thought.

"It's fine. I'm in Virginia, on a case. There's a spare key in my mailbox down in the lobby. The combination to the mailbox is seven-one-seven. You're welcome to stay there for as long as you need."

"Are you sure?" Danielle asked.

"I'm positive. Pack a bag and get to DC. I don't know how much longer it will be before I come back, but make yourself at home until then."

"Chloe…thank you."

"If you really want to thank me, you'll report the bastard."

"It's not worth it."

Chloe was pretty sure what she meant was it wasn't worth the trouble she'd have to go through in order to follow through on it. But they could discuss that later.

"Fine. Just give me a call when you're settled in my place, okay?"

"I will. Thanks, Chloe."

"Of course. Call me if you need anything else."

She hung up just as Moulton came walking over to her. He showed her his hand, which held two room keys. He then realized that she looked flustered and said, "Everything okay?"

"Yeah. Just…some stuff with my family."

"Anything bad?"

"I don't think so," she said. "Now come on…if it gets much later, we'll miss out on the tension of whether or not we're going to break our pact to keep things professional."

She followed him to the rooms, already rather certain the pact would be broken fairly quickly. With the case still looming over their heads and their one lead having been freed once his alibi had been verified, and now these issues with Danielle, she thought it might be exactly what she needed to refocus her mind.

***

Immediately afterward—no more than twenty seconds after Chloe had started toward the bathroom door to take a shower—she heard her phone ring. Still in her underwear, with her dirty clothes in hand, she walked over to the bedside table where her phone sat. She saw Assistant Director Garcia's name and answered it right away, feeling a little odd to do it wearing nothing but her bra and panties.

"This is Agent Fine," she said. She then mouthed to Moulton, still lying in bed and catching his breath as well, *"Garcia."*

"Agent Fine, have there been any significant breaks in the last couple of hours?" he asked.

"No. We had a potential suspect but that turned into a dead end. It actually turned into something of a small criminal matter here in town, actually. But the sheriff is handling it."

"Okay. Well, this is going to seem like it's coming out of left field and I do apologize for that. But I need you and Moulton to come back to DC. Specifically, Johnson wants to see Moulton in his office tomorrow morning."

"Has there been a break in the case?" she asked.

"No, nothing like that. I can't really address the reasons with you over the phone."

"Does Director Johnson need to see me as well?"

"Maybe later in the day. But no, you are not to attend the meeting between him and Moulton in the morning. He's to be there at eight o'clock sharp."

"Okay," Chloe said. She had tons of questions but could tell from Garcia's voice that he would not be answering any of them.

She ended the call and looked back over to Moulton. He was sitting on the edge of the bed now, a sheet covering the lower half of his body. He looked concerned. "Garcia, huh?" he said.

"Yeah. Calling for Johnson. They want us back in DC in the morning. Johnson wants to meet with you in his office at eight."

"Did he say why?"

"No. But he did say that I shouldn't come. Not until later in the day." She paused here and then suggested: "Do you think he knows about…us?"

Moulton shrugged. "Doubtful. Even if he did, I don't think that would be any reason to pull us off of this case."

Chloe wasn't positive, but she thought he looked incredibly troubled. His face was set in stone and his eyes seemed to dart everywhere, never staying focused on her.

"What is it?" she asked. "Is something wrong, Moulton?"

"No. I'm good."

She was pretty sure he was lying. He knew something…he was just choosing not to say anything about it. She decided not to pry, figuring that if there was anything serious, he'd tell her.

"Well, I'm going to grab a shower," she said. Then, almost as a test, she added: "I might need some help, if you're interested."

The smile he gave her was thin and forced. "I might sneak in later. But don't wait."

It was also clear that he *knew* she was on to him—that she had noticed that something was troubling him. Now, it was up to her to decide if she would leave it unspoken. For now, she figured it would be best left alone. If there was something he needed to tell her, they had a whole ride back to DC for him to do so.

She went to the bathroom and stepped into the shower. She wondered what Moulton could be hiding from her as she waited to see if he would join her or not. But as it turned out, she finished her shower alone, beginning to wonder what secrets her new lover was hiding from her.

CHAPTER THIRTEEN

"Are you sure you don't need to tell me anything?" Chloe asked.

They'd been driving for a while, a little less than halfway back to DC. Moulton was behind the wheel, staring out at the night-shrouded road with a set look of determination on his face.

"Let me ask you something," he said. "And it's going to sound confrontational but please know that I don't mean for it to be."

"Okay…what?"

"Do I know everything about you?"

The question took her by surprise. It also made her think of all the drama she'd been having as of late with her father and Danielle. "Of course not," she said.

"And even if we were closer…even if we'd been seeing one another for maybe a few months more, are there things about your life you still might not want me to know?"

"I'm not sure. Why do you ask? Moulton…what the hell is going on?"

He thought about it for a while and for a moment, Chloe thought he was going to come clean. But in the end, he shook his head. "I'll tell you tomorrow, after I meet with Johnson. You have my word on that."

"Fine," Chloe said, using a tone that indicated it was anything *but* fine. "Just let me know…I mean, is everything okay? Are you in some kind of danger?"

"No, nothing like that."

She did not like the cold edge he had to him; he was speaking to her as though she was annoying him, like he honestly didn't want to speak to her. So that's exactly what she gave him as they continued on toward DC—Moulton remaining quiet while Chloe tried to figure out whether or not she could fully trust the man behind the wheel.

***

It was well after midnight when Moulton dropped her off in front her apartment. She found herself wanting to kiss him goodbye but he was too preoccupied with his thoughts. He still seemed distant and cold, so she gave him only a quick "goodbye" as she got out of the car. He returned it, waved in a lazy and forced way, and then pulled away from the curb. She watched the car as it turned off onto another street, wondering what was going on in Moulton's head.

She then remembered that there was even more drama waiting for her in her apartment…if Danielle had truly taken her up on her offer. She hurried inside and went to the row of occupant mailboxes in the lobby. She opened hers and found it empty—mail, spare key, all of it.

Her heart started racing as she rode the elevator up to her floor. Danielle had never handled the harder things in life particularly well. That meant that Chloe could be in for a very long night of listening to her sister rage on and on about how her life had not turned out the way she wanted it to, how all men were devious pigs and how her life had started its downfall the moment their deplorable father had gone to prison.

Needless to say, when she unlocked the door to her apartment and heard '80s music playing, she was surprised. INXS was currently playing and when she entered the kitchen, she saw Danielle swaying back and forth as she cleaned off the kitchen counter. When she heard the door close as Chloe entered, Danielle wheeled around in shock. When she saw Chloe standing there, she raced to her right away and wrapped her up in a hug.

"I wasn't expecting you so soon," Danielle said.

"And I wasn't expecting you to clean my apartment," Chloe countered.

"I had to find something to do. I have all of this nervous energy to get out and let's face it…your counters are nasty."

"Sorry. I don't really have much time to clean." She reached in the fridge, grabbed a beer, and popped it open. She took a long gulp, as if the swallow itself would wash the tension of the last few hours away. "So, how are you?"

"Pissed off more than anything," she said.

Chloe noticed the red marks on Danielle's face. At least one of the slaps she taken earlier in the night had caused a slight welt.

"Did he come for you?" Chloe asked. "To your apartment, I mean?"

"Hell if I know. I got out of there about two minutes after I got off the phone with you. I just…I feel so stupid. The signs were there the whole time. And the more I think about it, the more I think he was giving me this business as some sort of front. He has money going around so many places and..."

"What?"

"Nothing. I don't even want to waste my time talking about the bastard. Let's talk about you for once. How have *you* been?"

There was the obvious secret she was keeping from Danielle: the fact that their father had come to her front door just two days ago. It was news that would hit Danielle with as much force as the slaps she'd endured earlier, but Chloe didn't see the point in keeping it a secret. Given what was going on with Moulton—whatever it may be—she felt like there were too many secrets in her life at the moment.

"I was doing great until yesterday. I came home and there was a visitor waiting for me. Danielle...Dad is out. He was sitting on my steps, waiting for me."

"Are you kidding me?" Danielle asked.

"No. For real. He was right there, just waiting for me. Asked if I wanted to grab lunch or dinner."

"Oh my God. What did you tell him?"

"I told him I wasn't interested. I told him if I ever wanted to see him or speak with him, I'd find his information and get back to him."

Danielle uttered a curse and nodded to Chloe's beer. "You got another one of those?"

Chloe retrieved another beer from the fridge, popped the top, and handed it to her sister. She noticed that Danielle was shaking slightly, the sort of tremors that run through a body when nerves take over. Danielle walked into the living room and sat down on the couch. Chloe followed closely behind, trying to be conscious of the fact that Danielle was going through a lot. Having been abused by a man she thought she loved and then finding out her father—a man she had spent most of her life hating—was now out of prison and free...that could be a lot.

"Talk to me, Danielle," Chloe said. "What are you thinking?"

"I'm thinking that it sucks that once the world starts to look good from a higher vantage point, that same world makes sure to buck you right off and remind you of your place. Chloe...I woke up this morning with my future looking better than I could have ever imagined it. And now...now all of *this*."

"I don't think it means much of anything that Dad is out," Chloe said. "I think he'll realize we want nothing to do with him and he'll move on with the rest of his life."

"If you want nothing to do with him, then why did you work so hard to set him free?"

It was a fair question and one that, on its face, was rather simple. "I knew there was something wrong with the way it all went down," Chloe explained. "I couldn't just let that rest. And when I started to dig, I slowly found out about Ruthanne…how Dad wasn't Mom's killer."

"He came to you, Chloe. He did that for a reason."

"Danielle…he *wasn't* the killer. And he *is* my father. I can't write him off like you did. But I also don't like the idea of just letting him back into my life either."

"I hope you know that I'm not hating him just because it's easier to hate him than to forgive him," Danielle said. "There are things you don't know…things I can't…"

Chloe reached out and took Danielle's hand. She could feel the shaking, light but definitely there. "You can tell me," she said. "Quite frankly, in our own family life and my personal life right now as well, I'm done with secrets."

Danielle shook her head. "No. I can't. I'm not ready."

"Danielle…you can tell me. He's out now. If there's a reason you're scared of him, you have to let me know."

She looked at Chloe, tears in her eyes, and let out a chuckle that was drowned out by the thickness of her tears. "Let's just say that the marks on my face right now are nothing new. And that my inability to trust men came from somewhere."

"What about your vagueness?" Chloe asked. "Where did *that* come from?"

The laughter was real this time, and Danielle wiped the fallen tears away. "Maybe someday soon, I'll tell you everything. But I can't right now."

"Please don't take this the wrong way," Chloe said. "But you being vague like this, it's make me assume certain things. And they're pretty bad."

"Assume away," Danielle said. "Whatever it is you're assuming, it's probably pretty close to the truth."

Chloe had nothing to say to that. She could only sit there with her sister, reflecting on how they had grown up with two different pictures of their father.

And wondering if he had been showing them two different faces.

***

69

Chloe woke up at 5:35 the following morning. Danielle was still asleep on the couch, insisting that she was not going to share a bed with her sister when she had no idea what her sister's sex life looked like. Although she hadn't had sex with Moulton in her own bed, Chloe was still afraid she'd blush, so she had not argued.

She thought of Moulton as she quietly made her way out of the apartment, not wanting to wake Danielle up. She considered texting him but recalled that cold distance he'd been giving off the night before. She figured she'd at least wait until after his meeting with Johnson to reach out to him. If he wanted her support, he'd ask for it.

She walked up the street to her favorite coffee shop, ordered a dirty chai, and then sat in the back of the shop. She Googled the number of the correctional facility her father had been released from, waited through the automated system, and then pressed zero to get an operator. Chloe asked for information regarding a recently released prisoner, only to be told that office hours didn't begin until 8:30. Chloe then explained it was for FBI business and gave her badge identification number. The woman was apologetic and told her that she'd do what she could to push it through as soon as possible.

"What exactly are you looking for?" the woman asked.

"I need to know the exact date Aiden Fine was released. And then I'd like to know the number of his parole officer."

"I'll do what I can to get that for you as quickly as possible, but it might not be until well after business hours."

"I understand," Chloe said, ending the call.

She sipped on her drink in the back of the shop, watching people come in and out. She again had to fight the urge to contact Moulton. She left the shop and walked around the block, listening and watching as DC started to wake up to a foggy Friday morning.

She was headed back to her apartment when her phone rang. She was fully prepared to be impressed, assuming it would be the woman from the correctional facility, having already gotten her the information she was looking for. Instead, she saw Moulton's name on the display. She answered it right away, trying not to sound too excited.

"Hey," was all she said when she answered it.

"Hey, Chloe," he said. She would never admit it to his face, but she loved to hear him call her by her first name rather than her

70

last—as most agents tended to do with one another. "Look, I'm sorry I was such a dick last night. This meeting...it could be bad."

"But you said you're not in any kind of trouble."

"Well, nothing life or death, no. But with less than two hours before the meeting, I feel like I need to tell you what's going on. I don't know for sure what the meeting is about, but I have a pretty good idea. I got an email from Johnson last night that all but confirmed it."

"So tell me," she said. "I'm not the judgmental type. I'd hope you know that by now."

"I do. But...how about over coffee? Somewhere close, because I don't have much time."

She smiled and looked back down the street where she had just come from. "I know just the place," she said.

***

It was clear just from looking at Moulton that he had not gotten much sleep last night. He'd apparently been kept awake by the stress of whatever his meeting with Director Johnson was about. He was dressed nicely, though, and had done his best to look presentable. When he sat down at the table with his cup of coffee, he looked like a man who was about to set out on a long journey.

"Thanks for agreeing to meet with me," he said. "After the way I behaved last night, I don't know if I would have if the roles were reversed."

"You *were* a little cold," she said, "and coming right after sex, it makes a girl wonder." She'd meant for it to sound almost comical but she knew it had fallen flat. "Besides...the moment I said we had been called back to DC, I knew something was wrong. Your attitude and mood completely changed."

He nodded, sipping from his coffee in an obvious attempt to delay the conversation. When he set the cup down, he had no choice but to go on. "Look...these past five weeks or so, when it's been sort of slow at the bureau, Garcia had me working with this small group that was tracking down this money laundering scheme...some set-up between a drug dealer out of Boston, a real estate agent in New York, and a bank here in DC. To tell you the truth, to this day, I'm still not quite sure how the operation was being run. But what I do know is that the group I was working with somehow got intel about where a shipment was being dropped." He used air quotes when he said *shipment*. "Now, these guys dealt in cash because it's ultimately harder to trace. And when they talked about shipments, it was basically drops...places where the money would exchange hands."

He stopped here, but Chloe had a good idea she knew where it was going. She had never pegged Moulton as a dishonest man, but still...all men had their faults and no one is perfect.

"We made three arrests outside of this drop. One was a pretty big one, a guy that had been wanted for electronic bank fraud for almost a year. But even more than that...we had the shipment in question. Right there in front of us, tucked away in these storage totes, in a warehouse in the middle of nowhere just outside of Boston. Including myself, there were four of us. And I can see by the look on your face, you see where this is going."

"How much was in the shipment?" Chloe asked. She wasn't sure how she felt about this. She wasn't even sure she should be hearing it; she felt like she was associating with a criminal.

"Six and a half million dollars."

She dropped her head and leaned closer to him. "How much did you take?"

"Each of us took one hundred grand. We thought it would be just small enough to go unnoticed. After all, no one had tracked the shipment. We were the first to find it."

"Then how do you think Director Johnson found out?"

"I have no idea. I haven't deposited anything. I've got it hidden...and I've been using that cash to pay for everything in the last few weeks, trying to slowly get rid of it, you know? I know it was stupid...but it was so easy. It was *right there* and no one knew about it."

"Some of the bills could have been marked or tagged in some way, I suppose," Chloe suggested.

"Yeah, that's what I'm thinking, too."

"Kyle...if this is what the meeting is about, and he has proof...this could be *very* bad."

"I know. But...I wanted you to know about it before the meeting. If it *is* what the meeting is about, then I don't know what happens after that. I didn't want to take the chance of not seeing you one more time before I get whatever punishment is coming to me. I had to tell you."

While she was indeed seeing him in a new light now, she also felt sorry for him. She had never seen him frightened before. She reached across the table and took his hand. "I get why you didn't want to tell me," she said. "And who knows...if there were four of

72

you involved, maybe the disciplinary action won't be as bad as you're thinking."

"An agent of twelve years got caught stealing just seventeen thousand dollars from a Russian money train three years ago," Moulton said. "He lost his job and spent eighteen months in federal prison. So that's the standard I'm looking at."

"Jesus, Kyle…"

He nodded and tapped nervously at the table. "Anyway, I need to get going. I just had to see you before I go. And I know it sounds selfish, but I hope you can forgive me for this. I think what you and I started here…I think it might have been pretty good. Pretty powerful. But if today goes the way I'm expecting it to go…"

He left the comment hanging there, as if speaking it out loud might make it a reality. "Wish me luck," he said as he passed by her. He leaned down and kissed her softly on the side of the mouth.

"Do you want me to ride with you to headquarters?" she asked.

"No. It'll just make it harder. Bye for now, Chloe."

And just like that, he was gone. She watched him walk through the door and back out onto the street, leaving Chloe alone in the back of the coffee shop for the second time that morning.

CHAPTER FOURTEEN

Chloe's nerves were shot by the time she got behind the wheel of her car and started to work. Her heart was breaking for Moulton, despite the obvious crime he had committed, and she also wished she could be there for Danielle while she hid out at her apartment with nothing to do. She recalled what Danielle had said about her own life the night before, about how one moment you were standing on top of it all only to have the world knock you on your ass and remind you who was really in charge.

She felt some of that as she parked in the garage and walked into the FBI building. She had woken up yesterday morning with Moulton still there, both of them feeling the beginnings of a potential relationship stirring between them. They'd then been called in on a case together, giving her an active and interesting case for the first time in almost six weeks. Her life had been on an upward trajectory, despite the jarring surprise of having her father show up unexpected on her doorstep.

And now look where you are, she thought as she nestled into her cubicle. She looked down the hallway toward Garcia's office, wondering if she might catch a glimpse of Moulton. She checked her watch and saw that it was 8:10. His meeting had already started by now, on the floor above hers in Johnson's office.

She tried answering emails as well as she could. She jotted down notes on the Lauren Hilyard case, thinking she might call Sheriff Jenkins later in the day to see if there had been any developments with Oscar Alvarez and his cousin. It made her wonder what would become of that case. Would Johnson send her back down there on her own or perhaps with another partner?

She tried to focus on all of these things, but it was too hard; her thoughts were solely on Moulton and what his future might look like.

When her phone rang at 8:37, she couldn't help but jump a bit. She grabbed her phone, hoping to see a familiar number: Garcia's, Moulton's, or even Johnson's. Someone to let her know what was going to happen to Moulton.

But the number was unfamiliar, though she *did* recognize the area code.

It was the correctional center—the place her father had been a resident of until recently.

"This is Agent Fine."

"Hi, Agent Fine. This is Tammy over at Somerset Correctional. I spoke with you earlier this morning. I have the information you were looking for."

"Thanks for being so fast," Chloe said.

"Sure, sure. Now, the inmate Aiden Fine was released two weeks ago. Apparently, some new evidence arose in his case and he was paroled out. As for his parole officer, it's a man by the name of Benjamin Nettles. Do you need his number?"

"Yes, please."

Tammy gave her the number and that was the end of the call. Chloe didn't even wait to consider her next step. She thought of Danielle last night, how she had started trembling when she'd heard that their father had been released from prison. How she had hinted at the fact that there were some secrets about him that Chloe might not even guess at.

She called the parole officer and he answered on the third ring. "Benjamin Nettles here," he answered.

"Mr. Nettles, this is Agent Chloe Fine with the FBI. I need the contact information for a man who was recently paroled. A man by the name of Aiden Fine."

Nettles obliged and as Chloe wrote down her father's phone number she realized that she, just like Danielle, was starting to tremble.

***

By eleven o'clock, Chloe's nerves were in such a state of disarray that she started to feel ill. She was worried about Moulton, still not having heard from anyone about the meeting. On top of that, she was currently pulling into the parking lot of a small Italian restaurant, where she had agreed to meet her father for lunch. The awkward conversation had taken place nearly an hour and a half ago but Chloe could still hear every single word of it in her head.

She walked into the restaurant, mostly dead from the early hour, and spotted her father right away. He was sitting in a corner booth, eating a breadstick and looking out the window. Chloe stood there and simply watched him for a moment. It had been years since she had seen him without bars or bulletproof glass between them—other than two days ago when he had showed up at her door.

Looking at him like this, he looked like a normal man. Not a home wrecker, not a potential murderer, not the monster Danielle painted him to be.

Just a man. Just her broken father.

She walked over to the booth and slid in. He looked up and smiled when he saw her. The smile was genuine and filled with enough joy to make Chloe uncomfortable.

"Thanks so much for calling," he said. "I was really worried you were going to keep your distance."

"I was, too," she said. "And I can't help but wonder if I have reason to."

He sighed and tossed his breadstick back down in the basket. "Even after it was proven that I wasn't the one who killed her, you still hate me?"

"I never hated you, Dad. Not even when I thought you did it. Not even when I found that you were technically innocent but were sleeping with the woman that *did*." She smirked and then, unable to help herself, added: "How *is* Ruthanne, by the way?"

"Well, that's something at least," he said.

They paused for a moment as a waitress came by and took their orders. Aiden ordered lasagna; Chloe got an Italian hoagie. They sat in silence for a moment, Chloe taking one of the breadsticks from the basket in the center of the table. She wondered if Moulton's fate had been decided yet. She wondered if Danielle's boyfriend had tried getting in touch with her.

It was odd how easily these thoughts came to her while her father sat across the table from her. She'd expected to be tense and always on edge in his presence. But there was something about his posture, even the way he looked longingly at her, hoping for some sort of conversation, that made her realize once again that he was not some monster. He was still her father despite it all, and she guessed things might always feel natural around him. She just wished reuniting with him could have been a little more meaningful—maybe even a little more emotional.

"How's Danielle?" he asked.

"She's doing okay," Chloe said, not even considering the idea of telling him the truth.

"I thought about going to see her…"

"That would be a very bad idea," Chloe said. "How would you even know where she is?"

"Do you?"

"Yes, I do."

"She living with a guy?" It sounded like an accusation rather than a question.

"Leave her alone, okay? She's not nearly as forgiving as I am."

Aiden looked as if he wanted to say something, but bit it back at the last moment. The waitress came by with their food, making Chloe realize that the silence they had originally been sitting in had lasted longer than she'd thought.

"Dad…"

It sounded weird to call him that as he sat directly across from her. While it still felt natural, she had to get used to the sound of it. "When we were kids, was there ever something that happened to Danielle? Maybe something between her and Mom or her and you that I never knew about?"

He thought about it for a moment as he dug into his lasagna. "Not that I know of."

It took everything within her not to tell him how Danielle had started to tremble and shake when she'd learned that he was out of prison—tried not to tell him how Danielle had insinuated that he had treated her in a way that was just as bad as anything Chloe could imagine.

"Why did you always prefer me?" Chloe asked.

He looked at her as if she had just fired a gun at him. "I never showed more affection to one of you more than the other."

"You did, Dad. I never understood it until later in life, but you did. You never really *avoided* Danielle, but you were distant from her."

Even as she said this, something started to present itself in her mind. It was a thought, murky and slow, like something dead in the water, slowly rolling over to reveal its pale belly.

"I don't remember ever being that way towards her. But then again…I wasn't the best father, now was I?"

"I didn't say that," she said. But she was only halfway present. She was trying to figure out the thought that would not quite come to her. There was something there…a repressed memory perhaps? Something about him treating Danielle differently. Something about privacy, maybe? That felt right but made no immediate sense.

"So tell me how you ended up working for the FBI," he said.

She tried a bit longer to get that memory to surface but it seemed stuck. So she did her best to appease him just enough to make it through this meal. Of course, she didn't want to tell him that it was her mother's murder and his arrest that had eventually led her to this career. So she gave a generic answer. Every question

77

he asked her for the next fifteen minutes, she gave him generic answers. She told him nothing intimate or deep about her life. When he asked if she was seeing someone, she told him, "Not right now." Which, as far as she knew, might very well be true now.

"Chloe...I need to ask you something," he said as he slid his empty plate to the side. "I'm not proud of it and it shames me to ask it."

"What?"

"I need to borrow some money. Not a lot, just enough to get me through the next few weeks. Unlocking bank accounts from almost twenty years ago is pretty tough. I have a tiny nest egg waiting for me at the bank, but it's harder to access than I thought...especially because your mother's name is on all of the paperwork."

Serves you right, she thought, a little guiltily. She did not want to give him the money. She didn't think he was lying to her, but it was the principle of the thing. Everything this man had put her and Danielle through...everything he had done all those years ago that had led to the death of her mother...

It also revealed the true purpose of him trying to tie things up with her. He cared nothing about reuniting or working on their relationship. He was only after a loan, plain and simple. She hated how much this hurt her—how betrayed she felt.

"How much?" she asked. Despite the hurt, she was fine giving anything to him. Maybe it would keep him away and she could finally move on.

"Maybe fifteen hundred? Just enough to pay the rent and get some groceries. As soon as I get that money freed up, I'll pay you back."

"Well, I don't have that kind of money on me. But my checkbook is in the car. I can write you a check if you like."

"That should be fine," he said. He truly did look embarrassed. "Thanks, Chloe."

She didn't bother with a *you're welcome.* In fact, she was too busy trying to think of a way to end the little daddy-daughter date without seeming like an utter bitch.

But as it turned out, she didn't have to think too hard. Her cell phone, sitting on the edge of the table, rang. She reached for it immediately when she saw Garcia's name on it.

"I have to take this," she said.

Aiden gave her a nod of understanding and started to look at his own phone.

"This is Agent Fine," she answered.

"Fine, it's Garcia. I came by your cubicle but you weren't there."

"Yeah, I'm out to lunch. What's up? Is the meeting with Johnson and Moulton over?"

"It is. And we'll fill you in just as soon as you get here. Meet us in Johnson's office as soon as you can. How far away are you?"

"I can be there in twenty minutes."

"See you then."

She ended the call and started to get up. "Sorry. I have to head back to work right away."

He smiled, also getting up. "Look…you're giving me a loan. Let me settle up the bill here."

Gee, thanks, she thought. She hurried out of the restaurant and got into her car, grabbing her checkbook. As she wrote the check for her father, every muscle in her hand screamed that she was being a fool. She was pressing so hard on the check that a black blot of ink came out as she finished signing her name to it.

She saw him coming out of the restaurant just as she placed the checkbook into her purse. She got out and handed him the check in an almost thrusting sort of motion—like the check was a dagger of some kind.

"Thanks," he said. "I really will pay you back. You just have to answer my calls when I reach out."

"We'll work on it," she said, wanting to make no such commitment. "Sorry again…but I really have to go."

She didn't wait for a response and didn't give him another glance. She got into the car, backed out, and headed out onto the street. As she headed to headquarters, she realized that she had the steering wheel in a death grip. Her knuckles were white and her jaw was clenched. She tried to decide if she was tense and angry over the lunch with her father, or because she was still clueless as to what had become of Agent Moulton.

Or maybe it was that memory from her past that had tried to present itself, only to sink away into the depths of her mind.

In the end, she decided it was all of it. And she did not relax or allow herself to breathe easy until she was parking her car in the bureau parking garage. But even then, it was sheer tension that pushed her forward.

CHAPTER FIFTEEN

When she entered Johnson's office, she saw that Garcia wasn't there. Johnson, however, seemed to be specifically waiting for her, standing behind his desk and looking out the window to the streets below. When he turned to her as she walked in, he had the same look she imagined someone might have when they had to break the news that a loved one has died. It made her heart sink.

"Chloe, I'm going to cut to the chase," he said.

"Okay." She did not sit down. Johnson was standing, so she would stand, too. Besides, there was too much nervous energy cascading through her to sit still.

"Agent Moulton got himself into a hell of a lot of trouble. As of ten thirty this morning he has been indefinitely suspended. He'll go to trial in a few weeks and if he's found guilty, he's looking at jail time. I doubt it will be anything more than a few months, but his career with the FBI will be destroyed."

She did her best not to seem devastated. She became angry with Moulton in that moment, wondering how he could have been so stupid. She could remember him saying *It was right there…* and explaining how easy it had seemed.

"Is he in the building?" she asked.

"No. he was escorted out of the building. He'll be allowed to return tomorrow with another escort so he can get his personal belongings." He sighed here and placed his hands on his hips. "Agent Fine, I need to you be honest with me here: did you know anything about what he was up to?"

"No, sir. He told me this morning, just before the meeting."

"Why would he do that?"

"Despite what he's being charged with might suggest, it's because he's an honest man at heart. He felt he needed to tell me because…I don't know. Maybe because he felt he owed it to me, as my partner."

Dodged that one, she thought. *Although, would it be the worst thing if Johnson knew the two of you were sleeping together? Hell, Moulton probably told him during the meeting. He probably had to come clean with anything unethical he's done while working for the bureau.*

80

"I thought he was honest, too," Johnson said. "And a damned good agent. This whole thing shocked the hell out of me."

"Same here," Chloe said, unable to keep all of her emotions in check.

"But despite what has happened with Moulton, I'd still like for you to take this Barnes Point case back up. I got a call from Sheriff Jenkins this morning. I had to call him back directly after the meeting with Moulton, actually. He says he has a potential witness…someone that claims they know who killed Lauren Hilyard. He's looking into the witness's story, but a lot of people in that town are still assuming it had something to do with Lauren's father and his friendships with higher-ups in Washington. I tried explaining to him that we feel that's not the case, but they are too scared and won't listen. Look, I'd brush him off if we were slammed with cases. But he seemed pleased that you and Moulton were there in the first place. He asked if you'd been pulled, but I assured him we'd send you back down there."

"Okay," she said. "When do I leave?"

"Soon. In the next hour, if possible. I'm going to send Agent Rhodes down there with you. She's just now really getting back on her feet and I think it would be a good exercise for her. Assistant Director Garcia is briefing her on the case right now. And honestly…with Moulton gone, she may be your long-term partner, anyway."

"Yes, sir."

"Jenkins speaks highly of you, Fine. Keep up the good work."

"Thank you."

With that, Chloe went back to her cubicle. She thought of Moulton and where he might be at that very moment. She wished she could have at least said goodbye to him. It was stupid thing he had done and she wanted to be mad at him. After all, his idiocy was ending the spark of a relationship they had started.

He's probably much more concerned about other things, Chloe, she thought to herself. *Let's not be selfish.*

She had to focus very hard to gather up her notes when she got back to her cubicle. Once or twice, she was sure she was going to start crying. Everything was piling up, pushing against her: Danielle's problems, her father showing up and asking for money, and now Moulton being pulled away from her and likely kicked out of the bureau. It felt cliché to be thinking such a thing, but she felt like everything was falling apart.

Just as the second wave of nearly crying passed, she heard a heavy knock at the edge of her cubicle wall. She turned in her chair and saw a familiar face there.

Rhodes was smiling at her, dressed in the suit she often wore into the field rather than the office attire she had been wearing for the last few weeks as she had gotten her feet wet with paperwork following her shooting. She looked confident. She looked ready to *really* get back to work.

"Hey, Fine," she said. "We ready to rock this thing or what?"

Chloe managed an honest smile. She fondly thought of how she and Rhodes had butted heads at first—small differences that had come to a screeching halt after Rhodes had nearly bled out in her arms after being shot.

"You know what?" Chloe said with stern determination. "I think I am."

CHAPTER SIXTEEN

The ride back into Barnes Point was uncomfortable for Chloe, but she did her best to hide it. She was genuinely interested in getting back up to speed with Agent Rhodes, but her mind was fixated on Moulton. She knew more information would come day by day in regards to what would happen to him. Until the trial, though, she knew there was nothing to do but wait and assume the worst.

The little bit she learned about Rhodes on the way back through Virginia was eye-opening. She had been tasked with research jobs, helping other teams locate information to push their cases along. She had also been assigned several jobs where she had listened in on wiretapped conversations regarding a sex trafficking operation that was suspected to have its central hub in Louisiana.

"It's disgusting what these perverts do," Rhodes said as she talked excitedly about the position. "Trading girls for a gram of coke, auctioning them off to the highest bidder for the night and then ultimately selling them for life to someone that will take them to some deplorable place in another country where they'll be rented out for the equivalent of three American dollars."

"Sounds like you're pretty passionate about it," Chloe said.

"I am. Which is odd because it was nothing more than a blip on my radar when I started with the bureau. I've been talking to Director Johnson about permanently assigning me to the task force that is working towards bringing that ring—and several other like it—down for good."

The closer they got to Barnes Point, the more natural it felt to be talking to Rhodes. As cheesy as it seemed, she wondered if there might be some sort of unspoken link between them, given the trauma they had shared just a few months ago. It had been a hell of way to start her first case—watching her partner get shot and nearly die on the way to the hospital—but Chloe understood that it had shaped her in some way. And as morbid as it may seem, she had Rhodes to thank for it.

"By the way," Rhodes said, "I'd be a total jerk to not say it…but I'm sorry about Moulton. It was out of nowhere, huh?"

"Yeah. It makes no sense. But…it is what it is. He regrets it and maybe he'll take some lesson away from it."

"For what it's worth, I'm sorry. Seems like you're on some deranged carousel of getting new partners."

Chloe gave her a smile, slightly forced. "Hey, I think I ended up with a good one."

Rhodes seemed content with that response. Chloe was pretty sure Rhodes was feeling some of the unease between them and this single comment seemed to dissolve it.

"So," Rhodes said, "Garcia filled me in, but would you mind giving me your perspective of the case?"

"Sure."

Chloe spent the remainder of the trip going over the case step by step. It actually did her some good, too. It helped her to step away from the drama she had been dealing with back home and to reorient herself toward the case. And as she talked it out with Rhodes, she started to get a better feel for the turn of events. She wasn't quite sure why; it was nothing that was absolutely concrete, nothing she could quite put her finger on.

And with that growing certainty in mind, she actually grew excited when she saw the Barnes Point welcome sign up ahead.

***

Sheriff Jenkins was out on a call when Chloe and Rhodes reached the precinct. However, the lady at the dispatch desk told them that he had been expecting them and had made things as easy as possible for them.

"He called my supervisor and said there was a witness in the Hilyard case," Chloe said.

"That's right. And she just happens to be in the back, speaking to a few of our officers to officially file the report."

"Fantastic. Can you point us in that direction?"

The woman got up from her desk and led them down the hallway. As they passed by the little room she and Moulton had interrogated Oscar Alvarez in the day before, a tiny flare of guilt shot through her. The receptionist brought them to the last office at the end of the hallway. She knocked on the closed door and it was answered at once by a slightly overweight cop with a handlebar moustache. He saw and apparently recognized Chloe, excitedly stepping to the side.

"Come on in," he said. "It's Agent Fine, right?"

"Yes, and this is my partner, Agent Rhodes." She looked to the table in the center of the room, giving a polite smile and nod to the woman sitting there. She looked to be in her late fifties, was perfectly tanned, and had her hair straightened to perfection. It was clear that she was from the Farmington Acres side of town. "Is this the witness?"

"Yes," the officer said. "This is Sheree Goodman. She came in this morning to tell us what she saw but is only now able to provide the time to fill out the report."

"Sorry," she said. "I had a work meeting this morning and this was the only time I had."

"Do you mind if we speak to her?" Chloe asked.

"Of course not. Help yourself. If you need me, I'll be up front."

The officer left the room, closing the door behind him. Chloe took one of the remaining seats at the table. She glanced at the report form in front of Ms. Goodman and saw that she was doing a very thorough job.

"Ms. Goodman, can you tell me exactly what it is that you witnessed? And then tell me why you waited so long to come forward with it?"

"Well, at first I figured it was none of my business, and I should keep my nose out of it. But then I heard there still hadn't been an arrest or even real suspects in Lauren's murder, so I thought I had better come forward."

"Okay, I can appreciate that," Chloe said. "So what exactly did you see?"

"Well, it was Sunday and I knew that Lauren was there by herself. Jerry goes in to his office most Sundays, trying to get things set up for the employees on Monday. He's co-owner of the print company, you know? Anyway…I just happened to be out on the back porch, firing up the grill while my husband was inside making burger patties. I just happened to look to the left, towards the street, and saw someone that looked familiar walking down the sidewalk on the other side of the street."

"And where, exactly do you live?" Rhodes asked.

"Farmington Acres. Four houses down from the Hilyards."

"And based on your knowledge of Jerry Hilyard's schedule, can I assume you know them relatively well?"

"Fairly well. Jerry would come over every now and then to watch Redskins games with my husband. But Lauren and I were never very close. The age difference and all…"

"Okay, so you saw this familiar person," Chloe said. "Who was it?"

"This young man has something of a reputation. He's a local guy named Sebastian Fallen. A younger guy...maybe in his mid-twenties, I'd think. Sometimes during the summer, he'd cut the grass and tend the ground at Farmington Acres pool, always with his shirt off. The teenage girls make such a fuss over him."

"So, it's not unusual for him to be in the neighborhood then?"

"He rides through from time to time. But it's rare to see him around on a weekend. I'll admit...I was curious. He looked like he was in a hurry and had his head down, like he didn't want anyone to see him. So I walked down the porch steps and went to the front yard, pretending like I was checking the mail from the day before. I barely saw him because he was moving so fast, but I saw him dart between the Hilyard house and the one to the right of it—the Andersons. And he was staying very close to the Hilyard house."

"You're certain?" Chloe asked.

"Yes. I even remember that he was wearing a black T-shirt with some band name on it. Rush, I think."

"What was your initial thought?" Rhodes asked.

"Honestly, I thought Lauren might be cheating on her husband. But I *did* know Lauren well enough to know that she's not the cheating type. She and Jerry were overly adorable together."

"You said this Fallen fellow has a reputation," Chloe said. "What sort of reputation do you mean?"

"Well, he's very sneaky about it and has never been caught or arrested, but there's many rumors that he's the go-to guy in town for drugs. I don't think it's anything serious...none of the bad drugs, you know? I've heard he sells marijuana and that sex drug, whatever it's called."

"Ecstasy?" Rhodes asked.

"Yes, that's the one."

"So do you think he was selling Lauren drugs?" Chloe asked.

"It's the only other thing I can figure. It makes more sense than an affair, but I don't even think Lauren was the type to do drugs."

"Do you know about what time of day this was?" Chloe asked.

"About noon or so. Surely no later than one o'clock."

Chloe thought all of this information over before getting out of the chair and heading for the door. "Thank you for your time, Ms. Goodman. Looks like you're doing a great job on that report."

Ms. Goodman picked up the pen she had been using and turned her attention back to the form. It was clear that she was filled to the brim with questions but was restraining herself. When Chloe and Rhodes were back in the hallway, they saw the officer who had greeted them coming down the hall toward them.

"That was fast," he said.

"What can you tell us about this man she saw…this Sebastian Fallen?"

"He's like a ghost," the officer said with a smirk. "We pretty much know he's selling drugs around town. Mostly pot. But we can never manage to catch him and no one will rat him out."

"Other than the drugs, do you think he's bad news?" Chloe asked.

"Hard to say. I don't know…a town like this, if he's busy selling pot and we can't catch him, I find it hard to believe he's into other things. Between me and you, he *does* sort of creep me out. We've had him in here twice for driving under the influence. He has this general attitude of not seeming to give a damn about anything."

"Has anyone gone looking for him since Ms. Goodman's story?"

"Not yet. Not enough hard evidence. Honestly, it might seem a little shady, but Sheriff Jenkins was planning to put a road check up about a mile away from Nelly's tonight, hoping to catch him. We figured we'd try to bring him in and then ask about what he's been up to this last week or so."

"What's Nelly's?" Rhodes asked.

"That would be one of the two bars in Barnes Point. Nelly's is on the other side of the tracks—the bar you go to, to play pool and hook up with people from high school that you used to hate."

"And Fallen frequents this place?" Chloe asked.

"Every weekend, he's a regular." The officer then looked at his watch and smiled. "Hell, it's almost five thirty on a Friday afternoon. He's probably already been there for an hour or so."

"Agent Rhodes and I will pay him a visit, then." *After the day I've had, God knows I could use a drink,* she thought.

"Need some backup?"

"I think we're good. But thanks all the same. Please let Sheriff Jenkins know we came by and what we're up to."

The officer nodded, watching them head back down the hall toward the front of the building.

As they stepped outside and headed for the car, Rhodes asked: "Is everyone in this town as nosy as Ms. Goodman seemed?"

"I wish that was the extent of it," Chloe answered. "There are weird friendships all through this town. People that were friends in

87

high school together are still friends well into their thirties and forties. The women especially...some weird little cliques."

"That sounds terrible," Rhodes said. "You know what doesn't though?"

"What's that?"

"The idea of heading to a bar on a Friday afternoon with the woman that saved my life. I think the least I could do is buy you a drink."

"Seems fair to me," Chloe said as she pulled out of the parking lot and headed out into Barnes Point in search of a sleazy bar.

***

Nelly's looked like any other run-of-the-mill tacky bars. A little hole in the wall place that advertised drink specials in the window with a simple letterboard. The Friday night drink specials were highballs for two dollars and pitchers of Bud Light for five. Dusk hadn't quite fallen in Barnes Point yet but the parking lot in front of Nelly's was filling pretty fast. One single look at the place before they even stepped inside, and Chloe felt certain that Jenkins and his men ended up out here at least a few times each weekend.

The interior didn't do much to improve Chloe's initial gauge of the place from outside. While there were "no smoking" signs everywhere, the place still held the stinking remnants of cigarette smoke from years past. The paint on the walls was tinged with it and the odor hung in the air like a ghost.

The bar was nearly filled, though there were only a dozen or so seats positioned along it. Roughly twenty tables—including four scarred booths—filled the rest of the area. In the back, three men were engaged in a game of darts while two younger couples were playing pool at an ancient-looking table. Currently, a pretty blonde was leaning over the table in an exaggerated fashion, her breasts practically falling out of her top. She was getting the attention she wanted as just about every pair of male eyes in the place were turned her way.

Chloe knew that it was irresponsible to drink while on the job but she also knew that she and Rhodes were clearly sticking out like sore thumbs. Besides, if things went well, they'd be out of here before they even finished their first drink.

"Grab a table," Rhodes said. "I'll get our drinks and ask the bartender which of these charming gentlemen is Sebastian Fallen. What's your poison?"

"A Guinness for me."

Rhodes nodded and headed to the bar. Chloe sat down at one of the booths, not wanting to be at a table in the middle of the place to draw more attention. She scanned each person and saw what you might expect to see at a small-town bar on a Friday evening. Mostly men, sitting at the bar and looking to the TVs behind the counter or to the drinks in front of them as if they were crystal balls. Other men, looking out of the bar's one window, perhaps pretending that the streets out there were streets in other cities—nicer cities they might never see. As for the women, they were all pretty much clichés, too. Pretty little girls, probably between twenty-one and her own age, clinging to those last remnants of being young. Trying to have fun and attract attention with their bodies. The one exception was a woman sitting at the far edge of the bar. She was a little overweight and looked sad—like life had been beating her relentlessly. She drank some kind of fruity drink and gave the liquor bottles behind the bar a deadpan stare.

Rhodes joined her in the booth with their drinks. Rhodes had also gotten a Guinness—another sign that maybe they were supposed to be partners, Chloe joked to herself. It made the pain of not knowing Moulton's fate that much more bearable.

"Did the bartender point out Fallen?" Chloe asked.

"No. But he said he had never seen us around here before. He also said we were both very pretty. And because of that, he guaranteed that Fallen would come to us in a very short matter of time…and holy shit, it looks like he was right."

She gave a slight nod to her left. Chloe looked that way and saw a man walking toward them, carrying a glass of what looked like rum or whiskey in one hand and a small tray with three shot glasses balanced on his other. If this *was* Sebastian Fallen, Ms. Sheree Goodman had been right. The young man was incredibly good-looking; his hair was disheveled in a good way and the five-o'clock shadow outlining his face made his dark eyes seem radiant somehow. She supposed when you looked like that, you probably had no problem being confident enough to approach two strange women with drinks.

"Hey, ladies," he said. "You mind if I join you?"

Rhodes bit back a smile. Chloe could tell that she was trying to decide whether or not to play the part of the bashful woman or keep her composure. Chloe, on the other hand, had no intention of pretending to gush over him. She wanted to get out of here as soon as possible.

"That would be fine," Chloe said.

Rhodes scooted over closer to the wall to give him some room. He then took two of the shot glasses off of the tray and gave Chloe and Rhodes each one.

"What's this for?" Chloe asked.

"You're not from around here. So I guess you're visiting. Consider this a welcome present."

"That's nice," Chloe said, taking the shot glass. She sniffed it and winced at the acrid aroma of straight tequila. "But I don't take shots from strangers. What's your name?"

"Sebastian."

"Well, thanks, Sebastian." She downed the shot and fought back a grimace. God, she hated tequila.

She saw Rhodes give her a shocked look which she then hid right away. She straightened up and pretended to psych herself up. She then took her shot as well, slid the glass over to Sebastian, and said, "Thanks."

"I mean this in the nicest way possible," Sebastian said, "but you two look too nice to be in a place like this. What made you choose to come to Nelly's? There's a much nicer bar on the other side of town…a lounge area and dinners and cocktails and everything like that."

"Those places are boring," Rhodes said.

"They are," Chloe said, sipping from her Guinness. It was much better than the tequila but she simply didn't have the taste for it in that moment. There was too much going on and she was hesitant to put anything in her body that might slow her down. "But those places don't tend to have people like you."

"People like me?" he asked, sitting forward and giving her a smile. It was a charming smile—a sweltering, sexy one, if she was being honest. Chloe felt confident that Sebastian Fallen went home with a different girl every weekend…probably a girl from this very bar.

"Yes," Chloe said. "You're Sebastian Fallen, right?"

"Yeah," he said, giving her a curious look. He was still so locked in his confident swagger that he didn't think to be alarmed that she knew his last name.

Very slowly, Chloe reached into her interior jacket pocket and took out her ID. She laid it on the table and opened it up. "We need to ask you a few questions, Mr. Fallen."

"Is this for real?" he asked. His eyes were wide and he was clearly alarmed, but the traces of that smile were still on his face.

"It's very real," Chloe said.

"What do you need to speak with me for?" he asked. He was suddenly very unconfident. He sat up straight and started sliding toward the edge of the seat.

"Just to ask you some questions," Rhodes said.

"Yeah, about what? The FBI in Barnes Point...seriously? What the hell is going on?"

"We just need to know where you were and what you were doing last Sunday."

Sebastian thought about it for a moment and then his eyes narrowed. He knew what they were looking for and his continued rigid posture made it clear that he wasn't going to give up the information easily.

"What is this about?" he asked. "Am I being accused of something?"

"We don't know yet," Chloe said. "That's why we're hoping you'll just answer our questions and make this as easy as possible on everyone."

"Last Sunday?" he said. "I was here and there and everywhere. I stay busy on the weekends, you know."

"Do you recall paying a visit to Farmington Acres?"

That narrowed look came over his eyes again. He looked back and forth between them, not quite in a panic, but heading toward it.

"Yeah, I was over there for a little while."

"Were you visiting someone?"

"Yeah. Well, no. Not really. I was over looking at the old push mower in the maintenance shed at the pool. I cut the grass over there during the summer, you know?"

"Well, it's coming up on fall now," Rhodes said. "Why the need to see the mower?"

"The blade needs to be replaced. And really, I'm trying to talk the cheapskate property owners into getting a new one."

"Was that the only place you visited?" Rhodes asked.

The panic was in his expression now. He slid out of the booth and stood by the table, trying to regain his swagger. "Look, if I'm not being charged with nothing, you can't question me like this."

"We can actually," Chloe said. She then leaned forward and lowered her voice into a conspiratorial whisper. "Sebastian, we know what everyone says about you. We know what the police even know but can't seem to get you tagged down for. And honestly, I don't care about that. If you're selling weed, I have to tell you that's against the law. I'd be a shitty agent if that weren't the case. But that's not why we're here."

He shook his head. "Tell me what it's about and maybe I can tell you."

She wanted to grab his well-toned neck and wring it. But she kept her cool, not wanting this to turn into a scene.

"We suspect that you paid a visit to the Hilyard house on Sunday afternoon. Right around noon. Is that correct?"

Again, just a shake of the head. "Nah. Wasn't me. I don't even know the Hilyards."

"Who *do* you know in the Farmington Acres area?" Chloe asked.

"Nah, I'm done," he said. That swagger was back but it was forced—just an act now.

He started to walk away and when he did, Chloe felt her cool not only slip away, but plummet. She was on her feet before she was fully aware of what she was doing. She grabbed his right arm, spun him around, and pinned it behind his back. She then pushed him against the table, the edge of it slamming into his stomach. He let out a whoosh of air and then bent over, gasping for breath.

Rhodes came in behind Chloe and applied a pair of handcuffs. Chloe looked around and was not surprised that every eye in the place was no longer on the scantily clad girl playing pool; everyone was looking at them.

"You made me make a scene," Chloe said. "And now, instead of answering questions at a table, over drinks, you can answer them from the interrogation room at the Barnes Point Police Department."

"Go to hell," he said loudly. "Both of you." He even chuckled as he said it. He was trying to gain face, trying to show everyone here at the bar—people he saw every week—that he wasn't fazed by this.

It took everything within Chloe not to shove an elbow into his defenseless ribs. Instead, she grabbed his shoulder and pushed him toward the door. Behind them, as the door to Nelly's drew closed, she could hear laughter and the murmurs of gossip. She wondered idly just how long it might take for the entire town to know that their primary supposed drug dealer had been taken into custody by the FBI. And, perhaps, even how long it would take before people started to wonder if it was about Lauren Hilyard's murder.

CHAPTER SEVENTEEN

Any lies or defenses that Sebastian Fallen had for himself fell apart the moment his pockets were emptied at the station. There were two ecstasy pills in a clear baggie and a rather unique-looking short pipe that reeked of pot. When these items were taken from him, there was no hint of that confidence and swag as he was led to the back of the station. Jenkins was back from his earlier call and when he saw Chloe and Moulton escorting Sebastian to the back of the station, a thin smile touched his lips.

"You mind if I join in?" Jenkins asked as they escorted Sebastian into the same room Chloe had led Oscar Alvarez into two days ago.

No…not two days ago, she thought. *That was only yesterday. Good God, the last twenty-four hours have been crazy.*

"Of course," Chloe said.

Jenkins sidled up beside her and whispered into her ear. "I've been trying to land something on this kid for two years now," he said. "You might have just done me a huge favor."

They entered the room, where Rhodes roughly guided Sebastian to the single chair behind the desk. Chloe wasted no time, standing on the other side of the desk and leering down at him.

"When people refuse to answer questions like rational human beings, it makes me think they've got something to hide," she said. "I told you: I don't care about you selling drugs. Right now, I'm more interested in why you were seen lurking around the side of the Hilyard residence last Sunday…the same afternoon her husband discovered her murdered."

Sebastian looked like a scared animal, backed into a corner. "You know, I heard someone killed her. Heard it was bad. But…there's no way I did it. You don't think it was me, do you?"

"I don't know right now," Chloe said. "Mainly because of the way you tried to get away from us at the bar. I need you to tell us right now what you were doing in Farmington Acres last Sunday…specifically why you were seen running behind the Hilyard house."

He looked to Jenkins, almost like he was looking for someone to back him up. He then looked down to the table, his eyes darting back and forth.

"Sebastian," Jenkins said. "I know you sell marijuana. Maybe other stuff, too. And we can deal with all of that later. I'll tell you this, though: the level of cooperation you give these agents might go a long way to how you're charged with the drug stuff. You understand me?"

"For real?" Sebastian asked hopefully.

"Yeah. I give you my word."

Sebastian sighed and then looked up at the agents. He looked frightened and a little ashamed as well. "I was telling the truth about the lawn mower stuff," he said. "I have proof of that, because I called the owner and tried convincing him to get a new mower again."

"But that's not the only reason you were in Farmington Acres?" Chloe asked.

"No. I went to the Hilyards' house because Jerry Hilyard had called me the night before. He asked if the rumors about me were true…if I was still selling."

"He was looking to buy from you?" Rhodes asked.

"Yeah. But it was clear he wasn't the type that had ever done something like that. I asked what he needed and he didn't know how to answer. He said he wanted something mellow, but strong enough that it would sort of serve as a relaxer. Something for pain."

"So why did you not go by there Saturday night?" Chloe asked.

"I wasn't in town. I was up in Farmville with this girl. So I told him I would get it to him sometime the next day. He said he'd probably be at work but I could leave the stuff on his back porch."

"And is that how it went down?" Chloe asked.

"Yeah. On their back porch, there's this ceramic frog, holding a flower pot. He left a little roll of cash there for me, and I left the weed."

"You never saw Lauren Hilyard while you were there?" Cloe asked.

"No. I assumed she wasn't home since Jerry had me leaving the shit on the back porch."

Chloe believed him, but it still left a lot of unanswered questions. His story placed him at the Hilyard residence sometime within a five-hour period when Lauren had been killed. But she also knew that it might be difficult to prove that he had left there directly after getting his money.

"Which did you do first? Drop the drugs or check the mower over at the pool?"

"I went to the Hilyards' first."

"How long would you say it took?"

"I don't know. Jerry asked me not to park right in front of his house...said he didn't want people making assumptions, you know? So I parked a few houses down and walked. Between the walking, getting to their backyard and then back to my car, it was maybe three minutes. Five at most. I don't know for sure."

"And did you go straight to the pool from there?" Rhodes asked.

"Yeah. You can check my call history. I call Mr. Hamlet after checking the mower out."

"How long do you think transpired between delivering the drugs and making the call?"

"I don't know. I looked the mower over pretty good. Maybe twenty or thirty minutes."

"What did you do after you left the pool maintenance shed?" Jenkins asked.

Sebastian froze here and started to shake his head. He gave Jenkins and both agents that hopeful look again. "Can this just stay in here?" he asked. "Like, does anyone need to know?"

"The only reason anything you tell us would need to leave this room is if we need to check your alibi," Chloe said.

Sebastian let out a little curse.

"What is it, Mr. Fallen?" Rhodes asked.

Sebastian looked at Jenkins with worry in his eyes. "You know the Shanks family that lives out there in Farmington Acres?"

"Yeah, what about them?"

"I went to their house after that."

"What for?" Jenkins asked.

"Me and Rebecca sort of have this thing...I go see her once or twice a week."

"You and Rebecca Shanks?" Jenkins asked, incredulous. He then turned to Chloe and Rhodes, a look of disbelief on his face. "Rebecca Shanks is married...has been for probably fifteen or twenty years. She's at least forty years old." He then turned back to Sebastian and added: "Where the hell was her husband?"

"He works out of town all the time. He's been in Europe for the last two weeks. We've been doing this for almost a year."

"Ah, Christ," Jenkins said.

"Sebastian," Chloe said. "How long were you there?"

95

"I stayed until about seven o'clock. I remember that for sure because that's what time her husband FaceTimes her every night."

Chloe looked back to Jenkins. "You know her well?"

"Well enough, I guess."

"You think she'll admit to this?"

Jenkins shrugged and started to pace the room. While Chloe could not put herself in his shoes, she could imagine what it must be like for one crime to dig up the dark secrets and sins of the town he called home.

"I can text her and let her know what's up," Sebastian said. "But...look, her husband doesn't have to know, right?"

"Not technically," Jenkins said, sounding disgusted.

"You know the locals much better than we do," Chloe said. "Sheriff, do you mind looking into that? And maybe following up on this call to the pool's property owner?"

"Yeah, I can do that."

Chloe had another question on her tongue but it was interrupted by the buzzing of her phone. She took it out and glanced at it. A surge of hope flashed through her when she saw that she had received a text from Moulton.

"Agent Rhodes, I need to take this," she said, gesturing to her phone. "Can you wrap up here and meet me out front?" Before waiting for an answer, she looked at Jenkins. "Is there somewhere private I can take this?"

"You're welcome to my office. Straight across the hall."

She left the room, already reading Moulton's text. It was simple and to the point: *Sorry about how it all went down. Doubt I'll get to see you anytime soon. Call when you get this if you can.*

She stepped into Jenkins's office and pulled up Moulton's number. She hated that she was so nervous, so angry and yet so desperate for him to somehow go free. She wished she could convince herself that she wasn't falling for him, but the jarring of her heart as the phone started to ring in her ear said otherwise.

***

"Thanks for calling," he said. His voice sounded softer than she had been expecting. She could not imagine the stress that he was under.

"Of course," she said. "How are you?"

"Scared out of my mind," he said. "I just wish there wasn't even a trial. If I'm going to be punished, I'd rather know right away what was going to happen. This waiting is punishment enough."

"Johnson was vague on the details," she said. "What are you looking at, exactly?"

"I'm suspended until the trial at the very least. And even if by some miracle the court goes easy on me, I'm still looking at some jail time. I have no idea how much. And I'm doing everything I can to not compare this to cases like this I've heard about from the past."

"I hear you're being escorted to the building tomorrow to get your stuff."

"Yeah. Escorted. Like I'm some massive danger to the people in that building. I understand what I did was a crime, but they're treating me like I'm a psychopath. I don't know for certain, but I'm fairly certain they've got someone parked outside of my building. But hey…that won't last too long. I may be placed into custody as early as tomorrow and held in a federal remand facility until the trial. Again…I won't know any of this for sure until tomorrow."

"Do you need anything?"

"No. I just wanted to make sure I got to speak to you. I feel like tomorrow is going to start this massive snowball going downhill effect. I have several meetings and all of these reports to fill out." He paused here, perhaps sensing that he was letting his despair run wild with his words.

"Anyway, how's the case?"

"It's moving, but a little too slowly. I've been partnered with Rhodes again and she seems excited about it."

"Good. I guess I should let you get back to it, then."

"Yeah…but Kyle…I mean it. Please let me know if you need anything."

"I will. And again…I'm really sorry. I was badly wanting things to work between the two of us. But I guess I made sure that won't be happening."

She didn't know what to say, so she let her silence speak for her.

"Anyway, thanks for calling," he said. "It was good to hear from you."

The line clicked in her ear, which was fine because she had no idea how to respond.

What had just occurred was much worse than a breakup. It was saying goodbye to someone, not knowing if she would ever see him again.

CHAPTER EIGHTEEN

It was 9:15 when Chloe drove back into Farmington Acres. Rhodes had asked if they should check out the Hilyard residence again just to validify Sebastian's story. With nothing else to do—other than go back home and obsess over what was happening with Moulton—Chloe agreed.

When she pulled up in front of the house, she saw that a few of the lights were on. She wondered if Jerry had finally found the courage to move back in and if the bedroom had been cleaned. Curious, she walked up the steps with Rhodes behind her. When she knocked on the door, she did so lightly, trying to keep in mind that there was likely a grieving man inside, trying to learn how to live in this house without his wife.

Jerry Hilyard did indeed answer the door. He looked as if he had just stepped out of the shower. He was dressed in a plain white T-shirt and a pair of gym shorts. He looked better than he had the day before but was still clearly not in a good frame of mind.

"Mr. Hilyard, it's good to see you," Chloe said. "I wasn't expecting you'd be here."

"I wasn't either," he said grimly, inviting them into the house. "But I figured I had to start sometime. It's only been a week and they are only just now releasing Lauren's body…but still. I felt stagnant over at the Lovingston house."

He led them into the kitchen where something was baking in the oven. It smelled like pizza.

"Has the room been cleaned?" Chloe asked.

He shook his head. "No. Someone is coming tomorrow to do it."

"Are you sleeping here?"

"I don't know. I might try the couch. But already…just showering and trying to scrounge up something to eat…it's weird."

"Well, we're actually glad you're here," Chloe said. "We've been working on the case and so far the only two potential leads have turned out to be dead ends. Just to verify the latest one, I do have a question for you: did you contact Sebastian Fallen last Saturday night?"

"Yeah," he said. "I did. Am I in trouble for that?"

"No. But…can we assume it was to arrange for the purchase of marijuana?"

He looked a little embarrassed, but nodded all the same. "Yeah. Lauren and I would use it from time to time. Nothing habitual or anything. We'd sit out on the back porch and have a joint on occasion."

"Can you tell me how you arranged the sale?"

"I asked Sebastian how much it would cost and I got that amount of cash and wrapped it up. Put it in the flowerpot out back, the one held by this ugly ceramic frog."

"And he delivered?"

"I think so. I mean…it was the following day, after the call, that I found Lauren. It wasn't until the next day, when the police were here, that I noticed the old ashtray out on the back patio table. The ashes were in there and the room had a very light smell of it. If the police noticed, they didn't say anything."

"Did Lauren ask you to make the call to Sebastian?" Rhodes asked.

"No. She only ever indulged when I did. I figured she'd be all stressed out from the reunion and it might help her mellow out."

"In the past, has Sebastian always been your resource?"

"Twice before. Before him, it was someone else in town…and I'd really rather not go down that road and rat someone out."

"How long ago would you say it's been since you used that seller?" Rhodes asked.

"About two years, I'd say."

"Do you know Sebastian Fallen well at all?" Chloe asked.

"No. I'd seen him here and there but that's about it. Seems like a good enough guy, I guess. A bit of a ladies' man from what I understand."

"Were the doors locked all day on Sunday?" Rhodes asked.

"I can't say for certain. They were when I got home. I remember having to unlock the front door. And the back door is almost always locked. But I guess Lauren could have forgotten to lock it back when she went out to get the pot."

"Do you mind if we take a quick look around?" Chloe asked.

"Help yourself. When you're done, there will be pizza in here if you want it. I just made it to have something to do. I'm not even hungry…haven't been since last Sunday."

They went to the back door and checked it out. Chloe had checked the doors the first time they had been here but she double-checked now; from both the inside and the outside, there was no

100

evidence of someone forcing the lock. Outside, Chloe swept her flashlight around the back porch and spotted the ceramic frog. She checked the flower pot in its faded green hand but saw nothing.

"Sebastian's not our guy," Chloe said, looking down into the yard.

"I was thinking the same thing," Rhodes said. "Just waiting for the sheriff to give us a call to confirm." She then nodded toward the back door, to where they could still see Jerry in the kitchen. He was sipping from a beer and looking at something on his phone. "You think he might remember something in the coming days? Maybe some detail he forgot about in the midst of losing his wife?"

"Hard to say. I just—"

The ringing of her phone interrupted her. She dared to hope it would be Moulton with some good news, but when she answered it, she was greeted with Sheriff Jenkins's voice on the other line.

"I just left the Shanks residence," he said. "It took some prodding, but Rebecca admitted to the affair. And the reaction I got out of her makes me think it might be over now."

"Did she confirm the amount of time Sebastian was there?"

"She did. She said he came over around one thirty or so and left around six forty-five."

"How about the pool owner? Did he confirm the call from Sebastian?"

"He did. So does Sebastian's call log on his phone. He made the call at twelve fifty-one and it lasted four minutes."

That still leaves about half an hour for Sebastian to have gone back to the Hilyard residence if he wanted to, Chloe thought. But honestly, she knew this wasn't the case. After all…he'd had an entire afternoon of sex with a woman almost twice his age on his mind. It was very doubtful he'd have committed the gruesome murder of another woman before heading over to the Shanks' house.

"Thanks, Sheriff. We're heading back to DC, but we'll be back to follow up." She ended the call and pocketed the phone.

"Back to DC?" Rhodes asked. "Why not just stay here for the night?"

"Honestly, I've got a family situation back home I need to check on. It's only an hour and fifteen minutes. Do you mind?"

"Not at all," she said. "So long as Johnson doesn't care. Is everything okay?"

How would I even begin to explain everything going on with my family right now? she wondered.

"Yeah," she said. "Everything's fine. Just…you know. Family drama."

She opened the back door and headed back inside the Hilyard kitchen. She was well aware that Rhodes was giving her a questioning look, but she chose to ignore it. For right now, a skeptical partner was the least of her concerns.

CHAPTER NINETEEN

When Chloe got off of the elevator and started walking toward her apartment two hours later, she heard the yelling right away. Someone was arguing quite loudly, raising their voice and using choice words. Chloe frowned, wondering how long it would go on. She just wanted to collapse in bed and forget about this day.

But then she realized that she recognized the woman's voice.

Danielle.

She ran to the apartment and unlocked the door. As she swung it open, she heard the voice Danielle was arguing with for the first time. It made her stop in her tracks for a moment, paused at the door.

"Dad, what the hell are you doing here?" Chloe asked as she closed the door behind her.

He was standing between the kitchen and the living room. Danielle was in the living room, nearly backed against the wall. She looked absolutely enraged, but at the same time, frightened out of her mind. Chloe had never seen such fear in her sister's eyes before.

"Chloe, I…"

"That's a great question, Chloe," Danielle said. "What the hell *is* he doing here? He said he had lunch with you…"

"Dad…you can't just come by unannounced," Chloe said, ignoring Danielle. "Especially when it's almost midnight. Why are you here?"

She took a few steps closer toward him, hoping to defuse the situation, when she got her answer. She could smell alcohol on him—something very strong, a smell that reminded her of the cheap bourbon he used to drink.

"I wanted to see you, that's all," he said. "But then I got here and Danielle was here, so…"

"I need you to leave, Dad."

"But I—"

"Oh my God, why can't you just listen?" Danielle asked, her voice still in that near-scream.

Aiden looked like he had something to say but swallowed it down at the last minute. He turned away from Danielle and then took one lurching step toward Chloe. The reek of bourbon was unmistakable now, as was the glossed over look of exhaustion in his eyes. He was very drunk and riding on a wave of emotion that had been pent up for almost twenty years.

"Dad…what's wrong with you?"

"I'm good," he said. "Paid the deposit on my apartment thanks to you. It's nice to be cared for and—"

"Not now, Dad. Please…Danielle and I need you to leave for right now."

"Yeah," Danielle shouted. "You can't just jump into our lives when you feel like it! I thought you'd be more comfortable on your own by now, you fucking jailbird."

Aiden frowned and looked at the floor. It was an expression that actually made Chloe hate him a little rather than pity him. "I messed everything up," he said. "Everyone I love just ends up hurting."

"Dad, you—"

"I'll call later," he said. He looked over his shoulder at Danielle one last time. Danielle turned away from him so he wouldn't see her crying.

He walked to the door, the only sound in the apartment his shuffling feet. He closed the door slowly behind him and when Chloe heard the soft click, she was glad he was gone. It was perhaps the first time in her life when she legitimately hoped she would never see him again. It broke her heart but it was also freeing in an odd way; it felt like finally being able to let go of her past.

"Chloe, what were you thinking?" Danielle asked, walking quickly toward the living room. For a moment, Chloe thought Danielle was going to hug her but she stopped short in the end and asked: "How could you have lunch with him?"

"Because I'm a sentimental sap," she said. "He showed up on my doorstep a few days ago and I sent him away. I felt bad about it so I offered to have lunch with him."

"How…how could you do it so easily?"

"It wasn't easy. But I thought about him being locked up for almost twenty years, maybe wishing he knew how our lives were going. Wishing he could see us. And I felt bad for him."

"You *are* overly sentimental." The tone she used indicated that this was not meant as a compliment. Not at all. "And he said you helped him pay his bills or something. His rent? Chloe, did you actually lend him money?"

"Danielle…I love you. But this is none of your business. It was my money and—"

104

"He helped kill our mother, Chloe! Of course it's my business!"

"Danielle..."

Danielle shook her head and marched to the far corner of the living room, where she had been keeping the single bag she had packed. She grabbed it up, shoved a few of her things in it, and then started walking toward Chloe—looking through her and at the door.

"Where are you going?" Chloe asked.

"Back home."

"Danielle, you can't. What if Sam comes looking for you?"

"He's easier to face than my father. And if he thinks he can just come by here whenever he wants, then your apartment isn't safe for me."

"Danielle, don't be stupid."

Danielle wheeled around and the look she gave her made Chloe's fists clench, going into defensive mode.

"I know you were his favorite," Danielle said. "And honestly, I prefer it that way. But in this scenario, you're the stupid one, Chloe."

Before Chloe could say anything else, Danielle was opening the door and storming out. Chloe instantly started to go after her but put on the brakes. She had seen Danielle like this more times that she could count: when she couldn't get a toy she wanted as a child, when their grandparents had not approved of the boys she had started to date at the age of fifteen, when they had first started looking into the finer details of their mother's death together.

She knew better than to go after her. And even if she did go back to Sam, Chloe had no doubt that Danielle could handle herself. She was not the kind of woman who would take shit from a man twice.

Still, as Chloe slunk into her apartment, she could not help but feel that she was letting everyone down. Danielle was disappointed in her, her father had unrealistic expectations of her, and she felt like she was absolutely nowhere on the Lauren Hilyard case. And while she had no hand at all in what had happened to Moulton, she couldn't help but feel like she was abandoning him.

Chloe crashed on the couch and simply stared into space. She looked to the corner of her apartment, where Danielle's bag had been until about two minutes ago, and wondered how it was possible for life to so quickly turn on a dime. It sent her thoughts toward Lauren Hilyard—a woman who seemed to have everything, a woman who had been enjoying her high school reunion one night and was then brutally murdered about twelve hours later.

If this job was teaching her anything, it was that life could be both beautiful and brutal. Sometimes it managed to be both at the same time. The trick, apparently, was to be able to accept them both in equal measure.

***

Around the time she and Danielle had started to unlock the secrets of their parents' past—at the same time news crews had started to park outside of her house—someone on Garcia's staff had sent her an email with information about the bureau's onsite therapist. It was something she had easily dismissed at first but had surfaced in her mind while she had tried to get to sleep following Danielle's departure.

She slept terribly that night. She spent a lot of that time wondering if all young agents just getting their start had to find ways to separate their personal lives from their jobs. Of course, she knew that her father's case had made her career something of a special case, but still…she knew she could not be an effective agent if she was constantly bogged down by her past.

Sometime between three and four in the morning, she finally managed to get to sleep. She jerked awake at six in the morning, though, as her alarm went off. She sat up right away because she knew the longer she lay in bed, the less motivated she would be to seek the help she felt she needed.

She ate a quick breakfast while she checked her email. She fought the temptation to call Moulton. She also fought the urge to call Danielle. It would do nothing but cause trouble and make things even stranger between them. She slowly got dressed for the day and as she drove in to work, she called the front desk and asked to be transferred to the bureau therapist, a woman named Mary Ziggler. She spoke with Ziggler's secretary and was able to nail down an appointment at ten o'clock. As soon as Chloe set the phone down, she found herself trying to think of a logical reason to call and cancel it. Of course, there was the need to get back to Barnes Point sometime soon. But all she'd managed to do there was to bust someone for potential illegal immigration and bring in a small-town drug dealer. Not exactly a case-solving performance.

As she was looking over the forensic files on Lauren Hilyard's murder, a familiar voice spoke up from behind her. "Barnes Point today?"

Rhodes was standing at the corner of her cubicle, poking her head in. She had a cup of coffee in one hand and her phone in the other. She looked about as tired as Chloe felt, making Chloe wonder what sort of night she'd had.

"Probably at some point," Chloe answered. "I'd really rather wait until we *know* we have something before we head back down there. The next time we visit Barnes Point, I'd like to come back to DC having wrapped the case."

"I get that," Rhodes said. "Sorry. I've been buried in paperwork for the last few months, recovering. The idea of getting out there and even just snooping around for leads is exciting to me."

Chloe nodded, not sure what to say. As an awkward silence fell around them, she noted that it was 9:55. "Can we get back to this later?" she asked. "I've got something I need to do at ten."

"Sure. You open for lunch?"

"I don't know yet. I'll text you."

Rhodes took this as a clear sign that Chloe was not interested in chitchat at the moment. Chloe hated to seem so dismissive but her mind was in a hundred different places. She and Rhodes gave one another a polite smile as they parted ways. Chloe went to the elevators and headed directly for Mary Ziggler's office.

She wasn't quite sure what to expect but it certainly wasn't what she walked into. Ziggler's office was really just like any other office. It was a bit larger than Garcia's office but smaller than Johnson's. There were two plush chairs against the wall, facing Ziggler's desk. When Chloe walked into the office, Mary Ziggler looked up with bright eyes behind small reading glasses and smiled warmly.

"Agent Fine," she said. "Come on in."

Chloe sat down in one of the plush chairs, taken a bit off guard by just how soft and inviting they were.

"I seem to recall," Ziggler said, "that I was given your name several months ago when your father's case was at your fingertips. I think some of your superiors were fully expecting you to pay me a visit. Can I ask why you decided not to?"

"I never really thought about it," she said. "I'm not one that really gushes her feelings out, you know?"

"Most people in your field aren't," Ziggler said. "So what's changed? Why have you come in today?"

"Oh…so it's just like that?" Chloe asked with a nervous laugh. "Right to the point?"

Ziggler reclined in her chair and returned the laugh. "That's another thing I know about the majority of agents—particularly ones in the ViCAP program: they aren't big fans of small talk. Though I can fabricate some if you like."

"God, no. No, right to the point is fine."

"So I ask you again," Ziggler said politely. "What brings you here today?"

Chloe started speaking slowly, starting with her father on her steps. She also mentioned starting a relationship with someone though never named the person. She knew there was a confidentiality agreement between the two of them but she still did not want to divulge the information about her and Moulton. She ended with the stagnant case in Barnes Point and the explosive scene between Danielle, their father, and herself the night before.

She looked at the clock on the wall and saw that getting it all out had taken exactly sixteen minutes. She was rather surprised; it had felt like no more than five.

"So it seems like you're being pushed to these great impressive mountaintops and then pushed down into dark valleys," Ziggler said. "Would that be fair to say?"

"Yes. Riding a high one minute and then struggling to even give a damn about anything the next."

"Given the way your childhood was, would you say it seems to be a pattern?"

"I don't know. I've thought about that. But once I got used to the fact that my mother was dead and my father was in prison, things were mostly okay. Aside from those two things, childhood was okay."

"The loss of parents to a child your age is sometimes an almost vague thing," Ziggler said. "Too young to grasp the totality of it but just old enough to feel the loss. It makes sense that you'd still be a little undecided about your father after all this time. You were never sure how to feel about his absence as a child and even now as an adult, with a better understanding of what happened on that day, it's still polarizing."

"That makes sense. But I need to know how to move past it. I need to know how to keep my feet on the ground I've found for myself. My career, my hopes and dreams…and not focusing so much on everyone else."

108

"There's no reason you can't do both," Ziggler said. "You're dealing with more baggage that most agents your age, you know. What *you* need to start to understand is that when your mother passed away, it did not automatically make *you* her fill-in."

Chloe felt like she'd been punched in the stomach. She sat up, a little offended but also a little dumbfounded. "I don't follow you."

"Tell me...why do you care so much that your father and your sister find some way to co-exist?"

"Because they're family. The relationship they have now is toxic."

"And that affects you, yes?"

"Of course."

"How does that affect you, exactly?"

"Well it...I can't...shit, I don't know. I hate that Danielle can't stand him. She talks about him like he's a monster. I sometimes think she might know something about him that she's not telling me."

"Replay all of that. Yes, they could be the sentimental worries of a stressed out sister—or any family member, in fact. But the need for preservation of one's family often comes down to a maternal instinct. Not that this is a bad thing. But I wonder if you have subconsciously been trying to play the role of mother in this family...maybe even while you were living with your grandparents."

I'll be damned, Chloe thought. *She's right.*

A million memories of living with their grandparents flashed through her head: her helping Danielle with her homework, helping Danielle clean her room, making sure any disagreements between Danielle and their grandparents were resolved.

"That's a good point," Danielle said. "I can even—"

Her cell phone buzzed in her pocket. She gave Ziggler an apologetic look as she took it out. "Sorry. I'm in the middle of a case and like I said, I'm not sure where my sister is right now."

"It's fine," Ziggler said, waving the apology away.

Chloe checked her phone and saw that the call was from Danielle. The fact that she was calling so soon after having walked out made Chloe think that there was nothing but bad news on the other end.

She answered it quickly, a little uncomfortable that Ziggler was sitting only a few feet away. "Hey, Danielle."

"Chloe, I'm sorry. I'm so sorry. But I need your help."

"What is it? What's wrong?"

"He's at the door. It's locked, but he's hammering on it."

"Danielle, call the police."

"I can't. Too much mess…he'll turn it to look like I'm the bad guy and…"

"Jesus, Danielle. Are you at your apartment?"

"Yes, and he—"

"Lock yourself in the bathroom. I'll be there as soon as I can."

As she killed the call, she noticed that Ziggler had straightened up in her seat. She eyed Chloe with a bit of concern. "Is everything okay?"

"I don't know," she said. And then, with a smile, she added: "This is one of those cases where the maternal instinct is just going to have to take over."

And with that, she sprinted out of Ziggler's office and headed for the parking garage.

CHAPTER TWENTY

Danielle's apartment in Reston was only a thirty-one minute drive from the bureau's parking garage—forty-five when traffic was bad. Because Chloe drove in a way where speed limits were only a vague suggestion, she made it to Reston in just over twenty-five minutes, pulling up in front of Danielle's apartment exactly twenty-seven minutes after she had left Mary Ziggler's office.

She ran into the building and up the first flight of stairs to the second floor. A small part of her wished that Sam would still be there but she found the hallway empty. Apparently, he had given up.

Or maybe he got inside, she thought grimly.

She had to fight instinct and not instantly reach for her sidearm. Even having her hand on her hip right now was not the wisest move. But she continued on, undaunted, to Danielle's door. It could have just been her imagination, but she thought she could smell the light scent of sweat and some sort of workplace smell like dirt or sawdust.

Chloe tried the door and was grateful to find it locked and in full working order. Apparently, Sam had been smart enough not to force himself inside. She knocked on the door, speaking right away to let Danielle know she was safe.

"It's me, Danielle. Open up."

She heard hurried footsteps right away, coming toward the door. The lock was undone from the other side and the door opened right away. Danielle wasted no time in coming to Chloe, giving her an awkward yet tight hug.

"Are you okay?" Chloe asked.

"Yeah. He just scared me. I thought he was going to knock the door down or something."

"How'd you get him to leave?" Chloe asked.

Danielle broke the hug and ushered Chloe inside. "I told him I called the police. He laughed for a while but he must have believed me. He left about ten minutes ago."

"Why was he here?"

"He told me through the door that he had been driving by, keeping a check. He said he saw me coming in the building last night. He wanted me back…wanted me to come home with him."

"How long was he banging on your door?"

"I don't know. Maybe fifteen minutes. I have never heard him that angry before, Chloe. That's the only reason I called you. He was…he was telling me about his other women. There are apparently two of them. He was telling me what they did for him and why—"

"Quiet," she said. "Don't even think about it. Don't give him the pleasure of it."

Chloe thought about what Ziggler had told her, about how she tended to lean toward some maternal need to take care of Danielle in a way their mother was no longer able to.

"You're coming back to my place," Chloe said. "And you're staying there until he gets tired of coming after you."

"I can't, Chloe. I treated you like crap last night. And if Dad knows where you are and—"

"Stop it, Danielle. Get your bag and come with me."

Danielle looked to be holding back tears. She actually looked like some fragile thing perched on a shelf, close to falling and shattering. Something started to boil up inside of Chloe and whatever maternal stuff Ziggler had been talking about started to morph into something else—something a little more prehistoric in nature.

"Where did he go from here?" Chloe asked.

"The new place…the one he's building for me. He's meeting with another contractor over there later today."

"What's the address?"

"Chloe…we can't call the cops on him. He'll tie me up in his legal mumbo-jumbo and that'll be a nightmare."

"What's the address?" Chloe asked again.

"One seventeen Nelson Street."

"Pack a bag. I'll be back in a while."

"Chloe…no. Don't go over there. He's mean and psychotic and just nothing but trouble."

She smiled thinly at her sister and said, "And things *didn't* work out for the two of you?"

"Funny," Danielle said. "But seriously, Chloe…"

"Give me half an hour. I'll be right back."

Danielle said something else, but Chloe barely heard it. She was already hurrying down the hallway, her blood boiling. She thought she had found an answer to the question that had been plaguing her for the last day or so.

How do you separate your past problems from the present?

You take action and you shut your problems down in your own way, one by one.

***

The front windows of the place Sam had been remodeling for Danielle were covered in plastic tarp. Still, she could see the figures of a few people moving around behind it. She parked behind a large work truck and stepped out. She walked into the place as if she had every right to be there. She caught a large whiff of the scent she'd smelled outside of Danielle's door: grime, dirt, dust, and sweat. The place was big, even with the stacks of lumber and unpacked furniture pressed tightly against the walls.

She had never met Sam before, so she had no idea who she was looking for. She approached two men standing by a sawhorse, a few boards, and a skill saw. "Excuse me," she said. "Would either of you happen to know where Sam is?"

"Back behind the stage," one of the men said, making very little effort to hide the fact that he was looking at her rear end.

"Thanks."

She walked toward the stage area at the back of the room, finding a doorway to the right side. This led her through a small hallway which emptied into a back room where a small table had been set up. There, she saw three men standing by the makeshift table—nothing but three large barrels and a sheet of plywood. All three men looked up at her as she entered. Two of them were dressed in work clothes. The other wore a casual white dress shirt and a pair of jeans.

"I'm looking for Sam," Chloe said.

"That's me," said the man in the white shirt and jeans. "Can I help you?"

Chloe approached him slowly, feeling all of her rage coming to the surface like lava. "Yes, there was something I needed to discuss with you in regards to Danielle Fine."

"What about her?" he asked.

Chloe threw out a quick right-handed jab that connected squarely with his throat. When his hands went up to his neck, she delivered a swift blow to his stomach. When he doubled over for this blow, she grabbed him by the back of the neck and pushed him hard against the wall.

The two men who were with him stood back in stunned silence. One of them was biting back a grin. Truth be told, so was Chloe.

113

She was so pleased with herself that it almost cost her.

He came springing off of the wall, clearly still shocked but trying to save some face. He threw a haymaker of a punch that nearly collided with her jaw. She blocked it, wrenched his arm backward, and then threw another punch that took him in the side of the face. As he stumbled backward, one of the men behind them had apparently seen enough.

"Hey," he said. "Wait just a damned minute."

He made the mistake of laying his hands on her. He grabbed her by the shoulders and pulled her away from Sam. There was some force to his grip but it was clear that he was not accustomed to fighting. He left his entire torso open, allowing Chloe to pivot, turn, and send her opened palm into his chest. He let out a comical *whooof* as he stumbled back and fell to the floor.

She turned back to Sam in time to see him coming at her again. He, too, was apparently not used to having to defend himself. He was coming at her in a hunched over football tackle, fueled by embarrassment and rage. There were about three counters she could easily dish out but she knew she could not hurt him too badly; he certainly wasn't worth losing her job over.

She sidestepped the attack while making a sweeping motion with her left foot. He went sprawling to the floor in a heap. Chloe walked over to him and placed her foot hard against his lower back.

"If you go to her apartment looking for Danielle again and I find out about it, I'll come back for you on an official basis," she said, showing him her badge. "And if you raise your hand to her again, I'll come back in n a very *un*official basis. Do you understand?"

Sam made a hacking noise through his hurt throat and responded by raising his middle finger.

Chloe drew her foot back and delivered a blow directly between his splayed legs. He let out a groaning sound as he slowly tilted over and fell to the floor.

"Hey now," the one remaining man said. "I think that's enough."

"It's not," Chloe said, turning away and walking back toward the door. "For men like him, it's never enough." She then looked back at Sam. He was wincing from the blow to his nether region and there was legitimate fear in his eyes. Chloe enjoyed the sight of it far too much. "Am I understood?" she asked.

"Yes."

"Say it then. I have two witnesses here. Tell me."

"I won't bother her again. You have my word."

He was trying to inflict some anger into his voice but it was quickly overridden by the pain and the fear. She nodded to him, looked at the other two men for a moment, and took her leave.

By the time she got back to her car, she started to understand that she could get into quite a bit of trouble if Sam reported this. But she doubted he would. A man like Sam would never want to admit that a woman had gotten the better of him—even if that women *was* an FBI agent. Therefore, Chloe wasn't too concerned. The only regret she had about the whole thing was that she had not invited Danielle to come along to watch.

CHAPTER TWENTY ONE

"So, are you not going to tell me what you did?" Danielle asked.

She had been quiet ever since she and Chloe had left Danielle's apartment fifteen minutes ago. She had never seen Chloe in such a mood before. She looked angry and very much in charge. For perhaps the first time in Danielle's life, she truly hoped that anger wasn't focused on her.

"I just let him know, in no uncertain terms, that you were off limits."

"With your mouth or with your fists?"

Chloe couldn't help but smile. "Maybe my feet, too."

"Thank you, Chloe. I hate to say it since it meant you having to beat the hell out of someone, but it means a lot to me. More than you know. But…you didn't have to do that. I can take care of myself."

"Oh, I know that. But I can help from time to time. I think maybe that's why things have always been a little strained between us. We never really want the other to help. But we have to get over that."

"Does that include coming to terms with how screwed up our recently freed father is?"

"I think it does, actually. But I don't want to talk about that right now."

This irritated Danielle but she didn't say anything else about it. She looked out the window to a sky that was looking slightly gray with rain clouds.

"Okay," Danielle said. "On to other things then. Have you given any more thought to the reunion?"

"Honestly, no. Danielle…this case I'm currently working on involves these bitchy women that just had their high school reunion. It's been a stark reminder of just how much I hated high school."

"All of it?" Danielle asked. "Even Jacob Koontz?"

"How dare you speak that name?" Chloe said with a smile. She hadn't thought of Jacob Koontz—the first boy she'd kissed and fought with her grandparents over—in a very long time.

"What's so bad about these women you're talking about?" Danielle asked.

"I can't give you details, of course. But it just brought to mind all of the drama and bitchiness. All of the cliques and how so many girls just buckled under the pressure of trying to fit in."

"Yeah, but you never cared about fitting in," Danielle pointed out.

"You're right, but I—"

Chloe stopped there as something dawned on her. Actually, it was more like something slammed into her, a thought that hit her like a brick.

We haven't paid enough attention to the fact that the Lauren Hilyard's murder took place less than twenty-four hours after the high school reunion. We spoke with Tabby North and Kaitlin St. John about it, but that was about it. Instead of looking for people that presently *have something against her, I wonder what we might find if we looked back twenty years or so to when Lauren was still in school. Even Brandie Scott claimed Lauren rubbed some people the wrong way back in high school...*

In other words: did something take place at the reunion that might have re-sparked some old high school rivalries?

"You okay?" Danielle asked her.

"Yeah, why?"

"You sort of went blank there."

"Made a connection about the case I'm working. That being said...I hate to do it, but I'm going to have to leave for work the moment we get back to the apartment."

"That's fine. I apparently need to do some job searching. With Sam out of my life, I'm currently unemployed."

"Are you...okay? Money-wise, I mean?"

"Yeah, I've got some saved up. You don't need to worry about me, Chloe."

"I know." The conversation with Ziggler replayed in her head, the insinuation that she was trying to play the part of the mother role.

"So...the reunion? You want in? You're not going to make me go by myself, are you?"

"You know what? If I wrap this case...sure. I'll go. I could use some distraction from the men in my life, too."

"Ooh, do tell," Danielle teased.

"I don't think so. Not right now, anyway." She cast a grin her sister's way and added: "Maybe on the way to the reunion."

Back at the station, Chloe and Rhodes were hunkered over a small desk in one of the extra conference rooms. Printed versions of the case files were in front of them, as well as all of the notes Chloe and Moulton had taken during their first tour through Barnes Point. Chloe had put highlight marks on several of the names.

"I follow you loud and clear," Rhodes said. "But walk me through this one more time before we hit the road."

"The tight-knit community of women in Barnes Point clouded my judgment," Chloe said. "The women are still so close after high school—even *twenty years* after high school—that we approached the case from the present. That's what led us to suspects like Oscar Alvarez and Sebastian Fallen. But when Agent Moulton and I spoke with some of these women—Tabby North and Kaitlin St. John in particular—they went on and on about their high school days. It's why they were so excited about the reunion in the first place. I think something happened at that reunion. I think something was said or insinuated and someone had some very old feelings of hatred or resentment take control."

"If that's the case," Rhodes said, "it would be feelings someone has been holding onto for twenty years. Unexpressed emotions that might have some surging out all at once. That paints a profile of someone with violent tendencies pretty easily."

"Exactly." She then picked up her phone and scanned through her notes.

"Who are you calling?" Rhodes asked.

"I'm going to see if Tabby North and Kaitlin St. John are free for dinner."

CHAPTER TWENTY TWO

They met Tabby and Kaitlin at a locally owned and operated restaurant in the heart of Barnes Point. Called Robin's Bistro, it was very upscale—almost pretentiously so. The steaks were thirty bucks a pop and the martini menu, which was three pages long, offered nothing less than ten dollars.

When Chloe and Rhodes joined them at a table by the bar area, it seemed as if the local ladies had already started drinking. They each had a martini glass in hand, each of which was just about drained. Chloe wasted very little time on the introductions, feeling as if this was the moment she had been waiting for—that moment she had told Rhodes about earlier in the day: the knowledge that this trip to Barnes Point should damn well be the last.

"I know you were both close with Lauren, so the questions I have today might seem inappropriate. And they may be hard to answer."

"Well, if they're super personal, your best bet is going to be to speak with Claire Lovingston," Kaitlin said.

"I figured that," Chloe said. "But because she *was* so very close with her, I fear her intense friendship would affect her answers. I need truth and honesty for these questions. Even if it means speaking ill of a recent murder victim. Are you okay with that?"

Both women looked hesitant as they nodded. Tabby drained the rest of her martini and slid it to the side of the table, an indication that she wanted another one.

"You told me yesterday about how Lauren was well liked in school, but that some people liked her more out of jealousy than anything else. I want you to think back to high school. Is there *anything* you can remember that she did…something that might be considered mean or cruel?"

"Well, you know, it was different times back then. You could sort of tease people and it wasn't called bullying."

"Did Lauren do anything that might be considered bullying by today's standards?"

"Well," Kaitlin said. She paused here, maybe wondering if she could keep going. She already looked guilty and hadn't even said anything yet.

"It's okay," Rhodes assured her. "Even if it's a bad memory of Lauren, we're hoping it might help direct us towards some answers as to why she was killed."

"Well, like we said…when Jerry Hilyard snatched her up off the market, most of the guys in school couldn't believe it. Especially the jocks. Now…I don't know if Lauren ever cheated on Jerry in high school, but I know she had lots of chances. And I know this because there were a few times when she sort of ridiculed the guys that tried to steal her from Jerry."

"Ridiculed how?" Chloe asked.

"She'd spread rumors about them. Nothing too serious, you know? Stuff about bad breath or smelly feet or bad acne. I think she did one time say that Travis Norris had a small dick. That one stuck for a while, if I remember correctly."

"What about Jerry?" Chloe asked. "Did he ever get ribbed by other guys because they were jealous?"

"Not at all," Kaitlin said. "When Lauren started dating him, he was bumped up to something like god status within the school. He was suddenly extremely popular."

"Would you say that Lauren was a so-called mean girl?" Chloe asked.

"I don't know," Tabby said. "Again…as snobby as it sounds, we were all friends so if she did, we never noticed or saw it that way. If she *was* being mean to people, it wasn't anything like enormous or deplorable. Nothing that would have made me stop to think…wait, maybe I shouldn't be hanging around this girl."

"These guys she made fun of," Rhodes said. "Were any of them at the reunion?"

"Travis Norris was there," Tabby said, starting to connect some dots. "And I think there might have been at least one more."

"You mentioned her talking to Brandie Scott and how that seemed a little weird," Chloe said. "Was there *anyone* else that might have been there who spoke to Lauren that you felt just didn't fit?"

"No," Tabby said. "Not that I can think of…"

"Wait," Kaitlin said. "She *did* spend a lot of time with the DJ. Like, up by his little booth. I figured it was just to request songs or whatever, but she was up there for a while, especially as she drank more and more."

"This DJ…was he also a student when you were in school?"

"Yeah," Kaitlin said, her eyes wandering now as she tried to remember. "But I think he was like a class above us. He was a year or two older."

"Would he have known Lauren when he was in school?"

"Pretty sure," Tabby said. "Everyone knew Lauren…even the guys in the classes above us."

"You got a name for this DJ?"

"I do," Tabby said, reaching into her purse. She took out her wallet, flipping through a few credit cards and reminder slips before selecting a single card. It was a business card, simple and cheap. There was a picture of a vinyl record on it, with a header: *DJ Scott Lambast – all genres, all styles – call me for your next event!*

The bartender came over as Chloe pocketed the card. He took Tabby's glass for a refill and then eyed Chloe and Rhodes. "Anything for you ladies?" he asked.

"Thanks, but no," Chloe said. "We were just leaving."

And with that, they gave their thanks to the local women and headed back out into the night in search of a local DJ.

***

Scott Lambast answered his phone right away and, though he was preoccupied with a wedding band he was part of, offered to meet them at the band's practice space. It was located in the basement of the local rec hall. When Chloe and Rhodes arrived, the bass of the band was ringing through the first floor. Even before they walked downstairs, Chloe could recognize the bass lines of Bad Company's "Can't Get Enough of Your Love."

When they got downstairs, the music was almost overpowering, encased in the concrete basement. The moment they entered, though, a man playing one of the band's two guitars stopped right away—apparently Scott Lambast. As he unshouldered the guitar, he looked to the rest of the band and gave a quick "Be right back."

He met Chloe and Rhodes in the back of the basement. He looked a little out of sorts, as Chloe supposed anyone might, having received a call from the FBI about a recent murder in the area.

"You guys mind if we do this outside?" Scott asked. He led them out a small side door that led to a thin wooden walkway. A yard sat below, with basketball hoops and a horseshoe pit.

"DJ and a band," Rhodes said. "You must stay busy."

"Music is all I know and all I ever wanted to do. And in a place like Barnes Point, you have to keep yourself busy to make a living off of music. Now…you said on the phone that you had a question about Lauren Hilyard and the high school reunion, right?"

"That's right," Chloe said. "We met with some of her friends and one of them claimed they saw the two of you speaking a bit longer than it would take to request a song. Can you remember what you and Lauren might have talked about that night?"

"Oh, sure. Nothing too serious. We were just catching up. I was a year ahead of her class, but like just about every guy in that school, I had a thing for her for a while. I asked her about Jerry—teased her about him not coming."

"Did you find it odd that he didn't come with her?" Chloe asked.

"No way. Not Jerry. He was never one to do stuff like that. He hated dances and events of any kind. I'm pretty sure the only reason he ever went to a school dance back in the day is because he had the prettiest girl in school on his arm."

"So, back to Lauren," Rhodes said. "Was there anything at all the two of you discussed—maybe even just something she mentioned offhandedly—that seemed weird?"

"Nothing that I can think of."

"Did she seem to be in a good mood?" Chloe asked.

"She didn't at first. It was obvious that she did not want to be there. But I guess she had a few drinks and the music was doing its thing. By the time things got into full swing, she seemed to be enjoying herself."

"Thanks," Chloe said, feeling defeated all over again. This was going absolutely nowhere.

"If you don't mind my asking, what exactly are you looking for?" Scott asked.

"We don't know yet. Anything that might give us a clue as to whether or not something occurred Saturday night that might have resulted in Lauren being murdered."

"Well, I don't know if it will help, but yet another thing I do in addition to DJing is to provide these flashy kind of videos of the events I DJ. I do it by setting a camera up on top of my DJ booth. It's tedious because I go through all of the footage to find the highlights. I've barely started the project for the reunion, so the majority of the footage is still raw and uncut."

"If you'd let us see that footage, that would be a tremendous help," Chloe said. "And the sooner, the better."

"Of course," Scott said. He then looked back to his bandmates and shrugged. "I have to bounce, guys. You guys mind locking up?"

They agreed, and Scott walked with the agents out the back side door and around to the parking lot. As Chloe got into her car, she heard the band kick into Eric Clapton's "Wonderful Tonight."

Scott pulled out ahead of them, leading them to his home. Chloe glanced at her watch and saw that it was 8:41 and had a feeling that it was going to be a very long night.

***

Scott Lambast had a nice little recording studio set up in his basement. Chloe assumed his time and attention to music came easily because he was not married. The house, while nice and warm, had the feel of a man who had never been married, a man who enjoyed the life of a bachelor.

He sat down behind a desk that was decked out in a small control monitor that was hooked to several speakers, some of the wires snaking into the foam insulation of the small recording booth in front of the desk. Scott did not look at any of this, though; he swiveled his chair to look at the large desktop monitor on the other side of the desk.

"How many hours of footage are we talking about?" Rhodes asked.

"About five hours, I'd think. Usually, when things start to get chaotic and just sort of a drunken blur, I shut it off. It's rare to get anything that's showable in the highlights from my videos."

"How many of these have you done?" Chloe asked.

"This will be my ninth. I did the reunion last year as well."

"So you've done enough of these to maybe notice strange things?"

"I'll say," Scott said. "This includes a rather blatant but well-hidden sex act between a boyfriend and girlfriend at the high school's senior prom earlier this year. There's apparently a lot that can be done when the guy wears his pants a little loose. But...I digress. Yes, I have something of an eye for things that are out of place."

"If you have a few hours to spare, we'd appreciate it," Chloe said. "An extra set of eyes never hurts."

"I'll do what I can," Scott said. He pulled up the reunion footage and pressed play. He then got up and walked elsewhere in the basement, leaving Chloe and Rhodes to view the footage. The footage was only a single shot, but it had been mounted high enough to get just about the entire room—what looked like a nice-sized dance hall. The footage began before the music had started. Chloe watched as a few people started to file into the room, most of them heading to the small bar area that had been set up on the right side of the room.

Scott came back with two other chairs, simple folding lawn chairs that creaked when he opened them. He offered Chloe his seat while he and Rhodes hunkered down in the lawn chairs. Together, the three of them started to view the footage.

"I don't even see Lauren yet," Chloe remarked. "Can we fast forward a bit until she comes in?"

Scott bounced to action quickly. He set the footage to shoot forward at three times the normal speed. The footage blurred by in this fashion for several seconds until a group of three women could be seen entering from the bottom left of the screen. "There she is," Scott said.

"And that's Kaitlin and Tabby with her," Chloe said. The fact that she had spoken to these women about going to the reunion with Lauren and now seeing it on a screen in front of them was enjoyable in a strange way. It made Chloe feel that they were on the right track now.

"It's always odd to watch the parties from this vantage point, from up high," Scott said. "You can see these little clusters of activity, different conversations, different emotions."

Chloe saw what he meant right away. She could see Lauren Hilyard, clearly there against her will, sort of hunched over as she spoke to a few people that meandered over to her and her two friends. Not too far away from them, two men spoke closely, as if exchanging secrets.

They watched in silence, the only conversation occurring when Scott asked if he could get them anything to drink. They both accepted waters and continued to watch. As they did, Chloe noticed what everyone else had been saying; after a few drinks and once the party started to truly get going, Lauren seemed to loosen up. She would laugh on occasion and, as the night wore on, tended to move farther and farther away from Tabby and Kaitlin.

As they watched Lauren's movements, Chloe noticed another woman. She was standing alone not too far away from the bar. She remained by herself most of the time, only being interrupted whenever someone approached her to talk. The conversations were always short and the woman remained in place most of the time. While her posture was a little angled, it looked like she was looking in the direction of Lauren, Tabby, and Kaitlin.

"Who's that?" she asked, pointing to the screen.

"Not sure," Scott said. "Melanie something, I think. I noticed her a few times. Sort of pretty, but stayed to herself. She sort of stuck out—not really part of a bigger group, you know?"

Chloe eyed the woman a bit longer. She wondered if this woman had been the type who had pretended to intentionally be by herself in school but secretly wished to be part of a larger group. The woman's posture and the almost longing stares made Chloe feel bad for her.

She continued to watch the scene play out and was able to spot the moment where Lauren and Brandie Scott spoke to one another at the end of the bar. After a while, Lauren moved away from the bar and headed to the back of the room, where the bathrooms were located.

She disappeared from the screen for a moment as she stepped out of view, toward the women's bathroom. Chloe watched the doorway, noticing that a lone figure was starting to inch along the back wall. It was a man, standing by himself. He moved slowly, as if inching himself toward the restrooms in a way that made it clear he did not want to be noticed.

"See that?" Chloe asked, pointing to the screen. "This lurker?"

"I do," Rhodes said. "He looks sneaky."

"That's Jason Morton," Scott said. "He was always a little strange as far as I'm concerned. I never knew him personally, but there were plenty of alarming stories."

Chloe almost asked him what sort of stories he was talking about but then she saw Lauren appear back on the screen as she exited the restroom. She made it maybe two steps before the man who had been lurking against the wall—Jason Morton—stepped out in front of her. Lauren stopped and did not try to sidestep the man. She spoke to him and when she did, they stepped close to one another, as if exchanging secrets. Jason then took a step closer and for a single moment, they were so close it looked as if Lauren had her head on his shoulder.

But then, as soon as they came together in what looked like an intimate manner, Lauren was shoving him away. It was a hard shove, but not a very exaggerated one. Jason staggered back as Lauren walked away, nearly storming back toward the bar. There, she got a drink and headed back over to Tabby and Kaitlin.

"You know if there's a history between them?" Chloe asked.

"I'm not sure if there's any truth to it, but yeah…I think there might be. One of those sort of high school legends, you know?"

"About Lauren and Jason Morton?"

"Oh yeah. This, I think, was before she and Jerry became a thing. A girl who looked like Lauren but wasn't offering up sex got a certain reputation, you know? Cock tease. The Blue Ball Queen." He paused here, perhaps fully recognizing his company, when he added: "Pardon the crude expressions."

"It's okay," Chloe said. "Go on."

"Anyway, Lauren did get caught every now and then messing around with guys. Either on dates or, once or twice, at footballs games, behind the stands. But because she was so well liked and pretty, it was seen as this sort of alluring thing. She was considered desirable rather than something worse, you know? Rumor has it that at some point during high school, she let Jason Morton feel her up in the back seat of his car…that she was about to go even further…but that he couldn't get it up."

"But you say it's just a rumor?" Rhodes asked.

"Yeah. A weird one, too. Because the Lauren I remember from high school would not have messed around with Jason. But she sure wasn't above slinging insults at people."

"The version of Lauren Hilyard I'm getting from the people I've spoken with paints a different picture. I hear she wasn't necessarily mean, just non-inclusive."

Scott chuckled at this. "I'm not so sure about that. She called some guy a fat ass during lunch one day, loud enough for everyone to hear. Even offered him a second chair to accommodate his large butt. She'd constantly make fun of sweaty guys in gym class. There was this one story about a guy asking her out…just randomly, you know. A brave kid, I guess. Rather than just saying she wasn't interested, she berated him in the hallway, embarrassing the hell out of him."

"I guess any friends she had wouldn't want to share that sort of thing," Chloe said. "Not wanting to speak ill of their dead friend."

"That, or the fact that they were just as bad sometimes," Scott said. "Anything not to seem different than their queen bee."

They were a little more than three hours into the video now. Chloe had gotten to her feet, pacing to keep her muscles from getting tight. Scott had put on a pot of coffee—also sitting in his studio space—and she was sipping from a cup. She now watched not only Lauren's movements but Jason Morton's as well. On a few occasions, he walked over to the exit doors and seemed to just float there. Maybe speaking to Lauren had irritated him enough for him to want to leave. Maybe he had been embarrassed all over again.

But then he slowly made his way back into the party. When he did, Lauren had made her way to the dance floor. She hugged to the outside of the dancing crowd, not doing much moving but remaining with a group of four or five friends. About halfway across the gym, standing near the back and pretending to engage in a group conversation with a few other people, Jason Morton was clearly visible. He was staring in Lauren's direction. In the footage, his face at something of a distance, it looked as if he were staring a hole directly through her.

Another half hour passed before anything of note happened again. Lauren and one of her friends walked over toward the bar. Jason, who had still been keeping tabs on Lauren, made a straight line toward the bar as well. He hurried his pace when he saw that she was about to get there before he did. When they crossed paths at the bar, Jason said something to her. He tried to get close to her again but Lauren stepped away. She responded to him in an animated way, speaking directly into his face and using exaggerated motions with her hands. Right away, a few people surrounding them started to laugh. Jason looked down to the ground, turned, and made a quick exit to the back of the room. He made his way to the exit doors and there was no hesitating this time; he hit them hard and left the reunion.

"Do you know if Jason Morton lives around here?" Chloe asked.

"Not in town, no. He lives in this little hole of town called Lovett. It's about half an hour outside of Barnes Point."

Chloe glanced to her watch. It was nearing one in the morning. She considered her options, wondering if they should wait until the morning. But her gut was telling her to move, to act on this right now.

"What can you tell me about him?" Chloe asked.

"There's not much to say, really. He's one of those guys that finished high school just to say he did it. He's worked a string of meaningless jobs since then. Clerk at a grocery store, cook at a burger place here in town, and, his most current job, inventory specialist at the Barnes Point Advance Auto Parts. There have been more in there, but those are just the ones I know for sure."

"He ever get in trouble with the law?" Rhodes asked.

"You know what?" Scott said, realization sinking into him. "I did hear some people talking about how he had been kicked out of a strip club in Richmond a few years back. Stayed in jail up there for a few days, I think. Locally, I don't know. He stays to himself. He was always like that, even in school. Which is why that rumor about him and Lauren Hilyard in the back of a car was so weird. Hell…maybe that's why it stuck."

"I don't suppose you know *where* he lives in Lovett, do you?"

"Sorry, no."

Rhodes followed Chloe and got to her feet. She let out a yawn and then looked almost admiringly at Chloe's cup of coffee.

"Mr. Lambast, thank you so much for your help."

"You want me to finish watching this to see if I notice anything else?"

"That would be a massive help," Chloe said. "Thank you for the offer."

She drained the rest of her cup of coffee, set the cup down on the desk, and then headed out of Scott's house.

"We going after him tonight?" Rhodes asked.

"I don't see the point. I say we go to the station, see if there are any records at all on Jason Morton, get his address, and meet him bright and early in the morning."

"Did you notice how easy it seemed?" Rhodes asked as they got into the car.

"How easy *what* seemed?"

"Well, that little altercation at the bar. Lauren was around people. She had an audience. And she gave them a show. And whatever she said got the response she was looking for. Sounds like the sort of person she was in high school, according to Scott. She slipped right back into that role a little too easily if you ask me."

Chloe only nodded, the thought striking her as profound. Perhaps Lauren had only fooled a few select people into thinking she had changed after high school. And if she had, surely it had only been for image management. And if that was the case, what had she been hiding about herself since graduating?

CHAPTER TWENTY THREE

Chloe pulled their car into Jason Morton's driveway at seven o'clock the next morning. He lived in a simple one-story house with a yard in serious need of some maintenance. It looked like the kind of house that had been in the town for decades, passed down by either family members or previous tenants who had gone elsewhere in search of greener pastures.

Rhodes, in the passenger seat, tossed the very thin file on Jason Morton to the back seat. Scott Lambast had not been wrong; Jason did have a very minor file at the Barnes Point PD. Three years ago, he had been brought in for questioning concerning a potential case of sexual misconduct at Barnes Point's rundown little bar, Nelly's. In a bit of a twist, another man who had been questioned about the incident had been Sebastian Fallen. In the end, neither man had been charged, though the notes in the file indicated that Jason's name had come up in a similar case a few years prior but the allegations had eventually been dropped.

His incident at a Richmond strip club was in the file as well. He'd apparently gotten handsy with a few of the dancers and after being called out for it, pushed one of the dancers. Security clocked him in the face and then escorted him out of the building. When he tried fighting security, the police had been called and he spent thirty-six hours in jail.

"None of this really screams *killer* to me," Rhodes said, nodding to the files she had just tossed into the back seat.

"No, but it spells…something," Chloe said.

They got out of the car and walked across a badly cracked sidewalk that led to the front door. Rhodes knocked on the door, the sound hollow and somehow loud in the quiet of the morning. There was a slight commotion from the other side and several seconds later, a muffled clicking as the door was unlocked from the inside.

A man's face peered out, tired and confused. A growth of thin beard outlined his face and his brown hair was in shambles. Chloe assumed he had just woken up.

"Who're you?" he asked.

"You're Jason Morton, correct?" Chloe asked.

"I am. Now, as I already asked, who are *you*?"

They pulled their IDs simultaneously, like some well-timed mechanism. "Agents Fine and Rhodes, with the FBI. We'd like to speak to you about Lauren Hilyard."

"Lauren Hilyard?" he asked, as if the name surprised him. "What the hell for?"

"We'd like to know what you two were talking about at the high school reunion last week."

Jason's eyes widened. He looked like someone had just read his mind or predicted his future. He'd clearly not expected them to know that he had spoken with Lauren at the reunion.

"Could we please come in, Mr. Morton?" Rhodes asked.

"No, I'd rather you didn't."

"I understand that," Chloe said. "But please know that I had a fellow in Barnes Point that refused to allow us into his home. He ended up in an interrogation room and we got what we needed anyway. So again…could we please enter your home?"

"Sure, I guess," he said. He stepped aside slowly, very uncomfortable as they passed by him. "I just woke up, though. And the place is a mess."

"I've seen far worse," Chloe said as they entered his house. The front door led them directly into a living room that smelled like burned bacon. The adjoining kitchen was in need of a thorough scrubbing but the place wasn't as bad as the exterior had led Chloe to believe.

"Mr. Morton, I'll save you the trouble," Chloe said. "We know you spoke to Mrs. Hilyard at least twice at the reunion. We know one of those discussions took place at the bar, right before you left very quickly. We also know that Mrs. Hilyard started a rumor about you in high school. So please be honest with us when you answer: what was said during those two conversations?"

Jason slowly sat down on his couch, frowning like a child forced to remember some particularly bad memory. "I'm not proud of it, but the first time, it started as just me saying hello and asking if we could put the past in the past. But it got sort of flirty pretty quickly. And I just asked her if she wanted to get out of there. But then she showed her true form…called me a name from high school that stuck because of her."

"Was the name a result of the rumor she spread about you?" Chloe asked.

"Yeah. They called me Limpy. Cute, huh?"

"Mr. Morton, was she ever overly cruel to you in high school?"

"Yeah, she was. She went above and beyond to insult me. Limpy…that stupid name still follows me around. If you know about the conversations at the reunion, I'm sure you know she shoved me. She called me Limpy then and everyone busted out laughing. Twenty years later and these people still haven't grown the hell up."

"Did you—"

Chloe's next question was interrupted by the ringing of Jason's phone—an actual landline. "Sorry," he said. "That's my supervisor. He's supposed to call me to let me know when I need to come in today. You mind?"

"That's perfectly fine," Chloe said.

Jason stepped away into the kitchen and answered the phone. He positioned himself around the corner of the kitchen that led into a hallway, the cord of the phone growing tight. Chloe listened in enough to make sure he was indeed speaking to his supervisor.

"Chloe," Rhodes said quietly.

Chloe looked to Rhodes and saw that she was nodding toward the small scarred coffee table in front of the couch. On the table, there were a few magazines—one the latest Sports Illustrated swimsuit edition—as well as the Barnes Point newspaper. Only a portion of it was showing, but halfway down the first page, Chloe saw enough of a smaller headline to gather what it said. She pulled the paper out and saw the headline, not the big story, but halfway down the first page.

Lauren Hilyard Murder Remains Unsolved, FBI on the Case.

Chloe didn't have time to truly look at the headline, though. When she pulled the paper out from under the magazines, she had loosened something else as well. It was a glossy Polaroid picture, featuring a young blonde woman—surely no older than eighteen, though that was a stretch. The girl was naked, lying on her back, her legs raised and parted while she did some self-exploration.

Chloe pushed the newspaper aside and found two similar pictures. The same girl was featured in each one. One of the pictures was focused on her naked breasts, the other on her exposed backside.

The girl was blonde and her face looked incredibly familiar.

The girl in the pictures was Lauren Hilyard…only much younger.

"What the hell are you doing?" Jason asked, now off of the phone and frozen in the kitchen.

131

Chloe drew her weapon and pointed it at Jason. She felt that it might be a little over the top and assumptive, but she was acting on pure instinct. It all seemed to add up, slowly but surely, toward a final answer.

"Mr. Morton, I need you to place your hands behind your head. You're under arrest for suspicion in the murder of Lauren Hilyard."

"Are you kidding me?" he said, his voice trembling. "Are you fu—"

"Now, Mr. Morton," Chloe said.

Jason Morton did as asked, his eyes darting back and forth as if looking for some way out of this. Rhodes hurried over to him and applied her handcuffs. He said nothing as Chloe holstered her sidearm and he was escorted out of his house by the two agents.

As Chloe and Rhodes led him down his front porch steps, they exchanged a look behind his back. It was a look of celebration, a look of *holy shit, that was kind of out of nowhere.* But Chloe was fine with that. She'd take a victory any way she could.

Besides, she knew all too well that normal-looking people were often the perfect disguise for heinous acts.

CHAPTER TWENTY FOUR

Following Jason Morton's arrest, Sheriff Jenkins and a few of his officers visited his home. Within fifteen minutes, they found a shoebox filled with similar pictures. All of the pictures—more than thirty of them—were of Lauren Hilyard at the age of seventeen. The majority of them were either suggestive or straight-out explicit.

When Jenkins handed them over to Chloe, he did so with a bright red face. "They were right next to his bed," he said. "Juts right there, out in the open."

Chloe nodded, taking the box. She looked through it, but only briefly. She had seen enough to know what she needed. It seemed to be the bright red neon sign she had been looking for, an expression of guilt. Or maybe they had been motivation, some final push to summon up the nerve in Jason Morton to do what he had wanted to do ever since high school.

Of course, she could speculate and assume all day and get nothing. She carried the box of Polaroids into the interrogation room. Rhodes followed behind her, her eyes glued to Jason in a vile way. It made Chloe think that if given the chance, Rhodes might very well slice this man's testicles off.

Chloe managed to keep her cool, though. She approached the table, sat on the other side, and very slowly, very deliberately, dumped the pictures out of the box and onto the table.

"Sheriff Jenkins says these were right by your bed," Chloe said. "I'll skip the vulgarity of asking *why* they were there. What I want to know is how you have them. And why they'd be out in the open so soon after Lauren's murder."

Jason did everything he could to *not* look at the pictures. He looked back and forth between Chloe and Rhodes. "It's sick, okay? I know it. But it's not illegal, now is it?"

"What's sick?" Chloe asked.

"That name...Limpy. I got it because Lauren told everyone about a problem I had. She and I...we really did see each other for a while, but in secret. She was ashamed of me. There was some overlap when she met Jerry. We broke it off eventually, but..."

"That still doesn't explain all of these pictures," Chloe said.

"Lauren made it clear to me before we did anything physical that she wasn't going to have sex with me. She said she'd do just about anything else, but not that. So imagine her surprise and my absolute horror when…well, when I found out I had an issue. They didn't call it erectile dysfunction when I was young, but that's what it is, essentially."

"So you never had sex with Lauren?" Rhodes asked.

"No. And I think my problem…I think that's why she stayed with me. She knew we could do all of this other stuff and it would never lead to sex. There were times when it almost happened…times when I was almost working like I was supposed to. But no…we never did. That's where the pictures come in. She let me do it. I think she got off on it. There were so many more than these. There were hundreds. But she asked for them back when we broke up. I kept some for myself."

"Even if I believed that story," Chloe said, "the timing does not sit well for you. We have you on camera, in a confrontation with Lauren Hilyard the night before she was killed. And then we find these in your home a week later."

"I swear…it's just coincidence. I saw her at the reunion and it broke my fucking heart all over again. I pulled them out and just…"

He stopped here and started to weep. But the tears and the choked back sobs were of anger. He balled up his fists and slammed them down on the table.

"That bitch ruined my life," he said. "Such a dumb thing…such a mean and immature thing. It ruined me. I wanted to hurt her…"

"Mr. Morton," Rhodes asked, "where were you on Sunday afternoon?"

"At home. Nursing a hangover. Getting those pictures out."

"You stayed at home all day?"

"No. I went out a bit after lunchtime."

"Where did you go?" Chloe asked.

Jason almost answered but seemed to understand where this was headed. A look of alarm crossed his face. Unable to look at the picture-covered table, he looked to the far wall instead.

"Where did you go?" Chloe asked again. "Mr. Morton…if you can provide your whereabouts and provide proof, you'd be free to go after some more questioning."

"Mr. Morton," Rhodes said, coming closer to the table now, "where did you go Sunday afternoon?"

He finally looked up at them and now the tears in his eyes were from more than just anger. He was broken. He was caught.

"Farmington Acres," he said.

And with that, he crumpled. He folded his arms on the table and laid his head down among the lurid pictures of the woman he seemed to have killed.

***

"He never made a confession."

Rhodes said this as they headed out of Barnes Point. She let the comment hang in the air, as if seeing if it sounded right.

"And I don't think he will," Chloe said. "Maybe at trial. But for now, he's still trying to hold on to high school. Trying to hold on to the dream woman that got away."

"Damn, that's sad," Rhodes said.

"If you really feel all that bad about it, we'll probably come back down in a few days if Morton still hasn't confessed. They can only hold him for four days without officially charging him."

"Oh, I don't feel bad for *him*. The whole thing just feels anti-climactic."

"I was thinking the same thing."

But the more time that passed—the closer they got to DC, leaving Barnes Point behind—the more certain she became that Jason Morton killed Lauren Hilyard. He murdered her because he had not been able to let go of the way in which she had hurt him in high school…and because she had chosen to continue to inflict those same wounds twenty years later. She had shattered an already broken heart and the result had been twenty years of pent-up rage and aggression coming out in a brutal murder.

Several minutes passed before either of them spoke again. It was Rhodes again and the question she asked took Chloe off guard.

"Were you and Moulton seeing one another?" she asked.

"Why do you ask?" Chloe asked, not seeing the point in flat out denying it.

"Because you're not talking about what happened. I broached the topic a few times and you shot it down each and every time. So, I was just wondering."

"Not officially," Chloe answered. "But all the same, it sucked to see him go through that."

Rhodes only nodded, apparently feeling that she had crossed some unspoken barrier. And that was fine with Chloe. As far as he was concerned, she, unlike Jason Morton, was just going to leave that hurt in the past and move on with her career—and her life.

CHAPTER TWENTY FIVE

"You're coming to this reunion with me and you're going to like it."

Danielle was standing at the kitchen bar, setting out plates for the dinner she had made them. It was an eerie comment for Chloe to hear; she assumed Lauren Hilyard's friends had said something similar when she had tried to get out of going to her reunion. She'd left Barnes Point the day before but it still seemed to cling to her—the case, the town, the peculiar post–high school friendships.

"One of those things is doubtful and the other is *highly* doubtful," Chloe said.

"Consider it a celebration. You wrapped this case of yours and I've managed to somehow unhitch myself from an abusive man that hid his demons well. I don't intend to just sit around your apartment and bemoan our lives over wine all weekend."

"Then don't," Chloe said. "You go. You have fun."

"I'm not going without you," she said. "And you know…Jacob Koontz will probably be there. And according to Facebook, he's single."

"He got married straight out of college, Danielle."

"Ah, but, as you well know, sometimes those right-out-of-college relationships don't work. He's been divorced for about a year and a half now."

"Since when did you start Facebook stalking the people we went to high school with?"

"Since I started considering this high school reunion," Danielle said. "I want to go in with some sort of ammunition."

Chloe considered it for a moment and sat down on the couch, facing Danielle at the bar. "I've only been back there once, you know?"

"I do know. But we're not going to go traipsing down some messed up memory lane or visit any surviving relatives. It's just me and you, some people we went to high school with, and a whole lot of alcohol."

Chloe thought it over for a moment. Would it really be all that bad? What would she do if she stayed home tomorrow night? She'd probably sit alone, thinking of what she had potentially missed out on with Moulton. She'd rack her brain with reasons to doubt herself about the case, to convince herself that Jason Morton was not the killer despite the fact that all signs seemed to indicate that he was.

"I'll give you two hours," she said. "If it's an awkward snooze fest where people are doing nothing more than comparing jobs and spouses, we're leaving."

"I'll take it," Danielle said, grinning far too wide. "I don't get it. You were pretty cool in high school. In that quiet, unspoken way."

"That doesn't mean I ever want to revisit it," Chloe said.

"You think there's something wrong with me for *wanting* to go?" Danielle asked.

"No. You were always a social butterfly."

"And you were always the caterpillar wrapped up in the cocoon, refusing to come out and see all the color."

"If that weren't such a great analogy, I'd be pissed," Chloe said. "Shut up with it already. I said I'd go. What else do you want from me?"

Danielle smiled as she looked around the apartment and then back to Chloe. There was a weight to that stare, thick with unexpressed gratitude. "Nothing else," she said, all seriousness now. "You've done more than enough already."

"Good. Remember that when I'm dragging you by the arm to get the hell out of there."

***

Their hometown—or, rather, the only town Chloe could clearly remember growing up in after moving in with their grandparents—was a two-and-a-half-hour drive away from DC. When they entered into Pinecrest, Maryland, everything came rushing back to Chloe. It was terrifying for her to recall just how close she had come to marrying Steven and living here.

As she drove through town toward the high school, she passed right by the road that led to the subdivision she and Steven would have lived in. She wondered what had become of the house they had moved into. Had he sold it? Did he still own it? Even considering such things sent a chill down her spine.

After she parked and she and Danielle stepped out of the car, she felt a strange synchronicity sweep over her. Lauren Hilyard had been walking into her twenty-year reunion two weeks ago to the day. Looking to the building that was housing her own ten-year reunion made Chloe feel almost dizzy. It was being held at the

Pinecrest Country Club, a building she had never stepped foot in while living in the town.

"You already look miserable," Danielle said as they stepped inside.

Chloe gave a fake smile as she opened the door to the country club and stepped inside. "No, no," she said sarcastically. "All smiles. I promise."

They approached a small kiosk just inside the doors. A man and a woman sat behind the desk, which held blank name tags and several markers. As they picked up the markers and started to fill them out, the man behind the kiosk made a little gasping sound and got to his feet.

"My God, it's the Fine sisters!" he said.

Somehow, Chloe had managed to push that unfortunate moniker out of her head. Once they had both started dating and word of Danielle's promiscuity started to circulate around the school, they had been labeled The Fine Sisters. Which was fine, seeing as how that was their last name—but it was the way in which *fine* was implied that had stuck. Fine, as in sexy or hot. Chloe had always resented it because she knew she had never been seen as hot when in high school. Not that she was aware of, anyway.

Chloe barely remembered the man, though Danielle was already wrapping him up in a big hug. Chloe stepped back and pretended to find something interesting in the hallway that led to the reunion's central hub just to avoid a similar embrace.

Danielle finally joined her, affixing her name tag to her low-cut shirt. Danielle had never been shy about showing off her assets and tonight was no exception. Chloe was happy for her, though; she looked cute tonight, and completely unaffected by recent events with Sam and their father.

"That was Malcolm something-or-another, right?" Chloe asked.

"Malcolm Price," she said. "He asked me out in tenth grade but I said no."

"Heart-breaker," Chloe said.

They walked into the large room that held the reunion. It was an enormous room, decorated to look like a rural lodge. Their high school banners were all over the place, as were balloons of navy and white, their high school colors. A DJ was set up in the far rear corner of the room, currently playing a Justin Timberlake song.

The next few moments passed exactly as Chloe had expected. She met several people she had gone to school with, a few she was actually delighted to see. She spoke with a woman who had been close friends with her through middle and high school; she'd gone to college in Alabama and had come home specifically for the reunion. It was the sort of commitment to high school memories that Chloe simply could not understand. Still, within her first hour, she and Danielle had somehow ended up splitting up. Danielle was talking to a few people she'd spent a lot of time with during her last few years of school (one of whim Chloe knew had once peddled cocaine and LSD through the school halls) while Chloe did her best to hold surface-level conversations with people who had been friends and, at best, passing acquaintances.

She checked her watch, fully intending to hold Danielle to her two-hour limit. When she saw that they had another twenty minutes left, she headed to the bar for her third drink of the night. She and Danielle had already reserved a room at a nearby hotel so if neither of them could drive, they were only a fifteen-minute cab ride from a bed to pass out in.

As she started on her drink—a poorly made rum and Coke—a hand fell on her shoulder. Her bureau instincts nearly had her grab the hand and wrench it around as she turned to face whoever was behind her. She pushed the urge down and simply turned around.

It was as if all of Danielle's teasing and prodding had manifested itself into reality. Standing behind her was Jacob Koontz—the first boy she had ever kissed, the first boy who had ever cupped her breast, the first boy she'd made cry when she eventually broke up with him. And in a cruel twist of fate, he somehow looked better than he had in school; his age showed, yes, but it had refined him somehow. In high school, he had the sort of face that could have starred on a family sitcom. Now, though, he had the sort of face that should have been on a *GQ* or *Men's Health* cover.

"Jacob," she said, very aware of the sizable grin spreading across her face.

"Hey, Chloe," he said. "I have to say…I did *not* expect you to show up at this thing."

"I hadn't planned on it. It all had to do with some nefarious dealings with my sister."

"Yeah, I saw Danielle when I came in. She made sure to point you out to me. She looks great." He smiled here, stepping a bit closer. "You do, too."

"Same to you."

Jacob stepped up to the bar and ordered a beer. As he waited for it, he turned back to her and grinned. "You know, I tried finding you on Facebook a couple of times but didn't have any luck."

"Yeah, I don't do Facebook. Too public. Too chatty."

"That's what I figured," he said. He then took his beer and raised it to her. "Good to see you," he said.

She clinked her glass against his bottle. "You, too."

"So what are you up to these days?" he asked. "I always assumed you'd end up doing something with law. Like an attorney or judge or something."

"Same ballpark, I guess," she said. "I'm with the FBI."

He laughed and then settled himself down quickly. "That's a laugh of utter shock," he said. "Not making fun. Because really…it makes sense. Are you like an agent?"

"Yes, I'm like an agent. How about you? What did you end up doing?"

"Well, I *was* a business owner until my divorce last year. My wife pretty much took the whole thing. So for the last few months, I've been a construction consultant…mainly for houses, but a few storefronts and things like that."

"Yeah, Danielle told me about the divorce. Sorry to hear it."

Jacob shrugged. "It was sort of doomed from the start, I suppose. Anyway…so, with the bureau…I guess you're living in DC?"

"Yeah. How about you?"

"Just outside of Baltimore."

And just like that, Chloe found herself slipping easily and naturally into conversation with a man who had nearly stolen her heart eleven years ago. That decade between then and now seemed like some huge chasm, though. It was hard to imagine her younger self talking to Jacob. But they had clicked in the sort of way that made both of them sure that they had been meant to be together, that they would last a very long time. She missed that naïve teenage love, but not the gullible person it had nearly made out of her.

They spoke at the bar for nearly twenty minutes, catching up and sharing their thoughts on current events, pop culture, and sharing high school memories—many of which involved their dating life. As they started to get truly comfortable, she saw Danielle walking across the floor, headed to the other side of the bar. She gave Chloe a sarcastic nod before glancing at a watch that was not on her wrist and then shrugging. Chloe rolled her eyes, but was unable to hold back her smile.

As she looked away from Danielle, she caught sight of a woman sitting by herself in a little lounge area across the room. Chloe could barely remember her from high school. She thought her name was Tasha or something like it. She looked quite uncomfortable, like she really didn't want to be there. It almost made Chloe feel guilty for having changed her tune so quickly.

"You okay?" Jacob asked. "You sort of spaced out there."

"Yeah, I'm good. It's just a lot, seeing all these people from high school and—"

Her name is Tasha Haskins, she thought suddenly. *She never really fit in and never tried. And she's doing the same now. Watching everyone from afar, wondering what their lives are like. Maybe hers is the same. Maybe...maybe you've seen someone just like her in the last few days...*

"Chloe?"

A thought dawned on her. It struggled to get out, wrestling through the haze of the three drinks she'd had so far.

"I'm good," she said, though she wasn't so sure she was. "Jacob, I can't believe this...but I think I have to go."

"Was it too much? Me just coming up and acting like ten years hadn't passed?"

"No, no...it's not that. It's a work thing and..."

She stopped here and grabbed a napkin from the edge of the bar. She borrowed a pen from the bartender and scribbled her number on the napkin. "Here's the proof I'm not just ditching you. Wait a few days and call me. I'd like to catch up."

"I would, too," Jacob said.

Chloe gave him a hug, her eyes already searching for Danielle in the crowd. She found her and broke the hug with one final goodbye to Jacob. It was harder to walk away from him than it should have been, especially with images of Moulton in the back of her head. She approached Danielle, who was currently awkwardly dancing with a few other women to a god-awful pop song that she *knew* Danielle hated.

"You look worried," Danielle said. "Is everything okay?"

"I don't know. Danielle, I just had a thought and...well, you're going to hate me for this but we need to go."

"It hasn't been two hours quite yet," Danielle said in a disappointed mocking tone.

"I know. I swear...Danielle, this is important. I think we might have gotten something wrong on the Barnes Point case and I need to get back to DC as fast as I can."

"Damn…you're for real, aren't you?"

"How much have you had to drink? Can you drive?"

"Two beers. Nothing strong yet. I can drive."

Chloe knew it was irresponsible, especially given her profession, but she didn't see where she had any other choice. "Thanks," she said. "Danielle, really…I owe you one."

Danielle said a few quick goodbyes and, to Chloe's delight, didn't seem to be too bothered to be leaving. In fact, she thought her sister looked a little excited to be driving her FBI agent sister back home so she could jump back on a case.

As Danielle pulled out of the parking lot, sipping on a water she'd taken from the bar before leaving, Chloe pulled out her cell phone. She called Rhodes first, feeling like a jerk to be making such a call at nine o'clock on a Saturday night. When Rhodes answered, she sounded slightly bored, yet glad to hear from Chloe.

"Sorry to bother you so late on a Saturday, but I think we might need to meet up. I think we might need to go back to Barnes Point."

"What the hell for?"

Chloe told her the thoughts that had gone parading through her head. Rhodes sounded convinced, almost in an excited sort of state by the time they ended the call. She then immediately made her next call, not expecting an answer, but hoping for the best. The call was answered on the third ring. When the person on the other end answered it, his voice was almost entirely drowned out by loud, blaring music.

"Scott? It's Agent Fine. From the sound of it, you're on the job."

"I am. What can I do for you?"

"Is there any way possible that we could meet up at your studio? I want to take another look at that video of the reunion."

"Give me an hour. I've got a backup I can bring in to relieve me."

Chloe gave her thanks and ended the call. She looked to the road, then to her sister.

"You sure you're sober?" Chloe asked.

"If I wasn't before, I am now. Hearing you on the phone like that, it's sort of exciting. I feel like a sidekick."

"That's exactly what you are. But as a sidekick, your partner is an FBI agent. That means you can speed it up a bit."

Danielle grinned and did as she was asked. The reunion nothing more than an afterthought in their heads, Danielle sped them back toward DC while Chloe looked back over the case, wondering how she and Rhodes had missed something so obvious.

CHAPTER TWENTY SIX

Scott Lambast seemed as if he felt very much like Danielle had felt; excited and eager to help out on the case in any way he could. By the time Chloe and Rhodes appeared at his house just shy of midnight, he had already settled down in his studio and pulled the footage up. He had paused it at the scene where Jason Morton could be seen lurking against the back wall, as if waiting for Lauren Hilyard to come back out.

"I figured this is where you'd want to pick it up," Scott said.

"A good thought," Chloe said, "but I need to go backwards a little bit."

Scott did as he was asked and cycled back through the footage. It took about twenty seconds for him to get to the spot she wanted. "Right there," she said, stepping forward and pointing at the screen—to the lonely woman at the end of the bar.

"You said her name was Melanie, right?" Rhodes asked.

"Yeah," Scott answered. "But I don't know about a last name. At the risk of sounding like a putz, I never really paid much attention to her in school."

Yeah, I bet no one ever did, Chloe thought.

Chloe watched Melanie for the next several minutes. She spent a lot of her time looking painfully in the direction of several different groups. But her eyes almost always drifted back to Lauren. Even when Lauren was separated from her group of primary friends like Tabby and Kaitlin, Melanie seemed to track her.

"Skip ahead a bit," Chloe said.

Scott fast forwarded the scene, Chloe keeping her eyes on Melanie. She stayed against that one side of the room, as if she were using the bar as a sort of base. She didn't drink that much; as far as Chloe could tell, she only had two drinks the entire time. When she finally did move away from the wall and started across the room, Chloe placed a hand on Scott's shoulder. "Stop it right there."

The screen went back to normal speed as Melanie seemed to be walking in the direction of Lauren and another woman. She got halfway across the room and came to a stop. She seemed to consider something for a moment before turning and walking to the back of the room toward the restroom. When she walked into the ladies' room, she stayed there for quite a while. Eight minutes passed by, most of which Scott fast-forwarded through, until she came back. When she reappeared, someone approached her and spoke with her briefly. But it was clear that Melanie was not interested.

Within a few minutes, she was back to stalking around the crowd. She blended in well; she did it in a way that suggested she had been doing it her whole life.

"Do you have the capabilities to print a screenshot of this out?" Chloe asked.

"The best I can do is get a screen grab and save it as a JPEG."

"That'll do."

As Scott worked at doing this, Rhodes and Chloe adjourned to the back of the studio. Rhodes took one final look back at the screen, where Scott had paused the video again.

"I know it seems like a stretch," Chloe said. "But it sort of fits, doesn't it? The girl that was never really seen by anyone in high school. Envious of the popular girl. Rhodes, did you see how intently she's staring at Lauren in that video?"

"I did. It *was* sort of creepy."

"We have to talk to her. And even if she does nothing more than give us more terrible stories about how Lauren Hilyard treated people in high school, I feel like someone that drawn to Lauren could either strengthen the case against Jason Morton or show the holes in it."

"But you don't think Jason did it anymore?"

"I don't know. The way he had those pictures…it was pretty sad and perverted but there was nothing in them to suggest he wanted to see her hurt. He was objectifying her by looking back at those pictures, sure, but…"

"But a man that wanted her dead wouldn't be appreciating her body in such a way."

Chloe nodded. It had been the one thing that had not sat well with her since they had arrested Jason Morton. It had not seemed to fit with the profile she had been putting together in her head.

"I've got your picture printing out," Scott said. "But if you don't mind my asking, how are you even going to find her based off of this one picture?"

It was a good question, but Chloe already had a few ideas.

***

Nelly's was in high gear when Rhodes parked the car in the crowded parking lot. Even before they got out of the car, they could hear the bass of some shit-kicking country song coming from within the bar. They exchanged a slightly disgusted glance over the roof of the car as they headed inside.

Chloe sized up the room, a little taken aback at just how packed it was. She started to look around for people who looked to be between twenty-eight and thirty but found it harder than it should have been. She figured the best thing to do would be going to the expert. She walked directly to the bar and spotted the bartender who had been here when she and Rhodes had questioned Sebastian Fallen.

"Hey," the bartender said cautiously. "I'm not looking for another scene."

"We're not, either," Chloe said. "You know who Lauren Hilyard is?"

"Yeah. She was killed two weeks ago, right? Married to Jerry Hilyard. People still talk about how she was hot stuff in high school."

"That's right. Can you point out anyone in here that might have graduated in the same class as her?"

"Well hell...yeah, that's easy." He nodded directly behind them, to a small table where a man was sitting by himself. It was a man Chloe recognized—a man she had seen quite recently, in fact.

Jerry Hilyard looked like he might fall off of the chair he was sitting in. He had both hands wrapped around a mug of beer, looking down into it as if there might be tea leaves (or, in this case, hops leaves) to be read.

"How long has he been in here?" Rhodes asked.

"A while. Since at least nine. A few people have gone up to him to be polite. Offer their condolences and all. But he clearly just wants to be left alone, you know? He came in, ordered his first beer, and asked to keep an open tab...and to make sure he never had an empty beer on his table until he left. I told him I could do that, but he'd need to leave me his keys. He did, and I have a cab company number ready to go."

"How many drinks in is he?"

The bartender shrugged. "I'm not sure. Eight? Maybe nine."

Chloe thanked the bartender and then slowly made her way over to Jerry. Rhodes followed behind, eliciting at least one catcall as she did so.

Chloe stopped at the table and took the open seat across from him. He looked up at her and it took a moment for him to recognize her. He nodded as if she had said something and then looked at his surroundings.

"Not my finest moment," he said. His words were slow, and he enunciated each one carefully. "I wanted to be out around people...but all people want to do is tell me how sorry they are."

"Mr. Hilyard, are you okay?"

She had to raise her voice to be heard over the music. She hated herself a bit for recognizing the song. "Fast as You" by Dwight Yoakam.

"Sure," Jerry said. "Neither of my kids want to come home. Even after the funeral...they wanted nothing to do with me. Lauren's parents think it's just too painful here right now for them. But they never asked how I was doing. Assholes are probably glad she's dead just so she can't be with me anymore."

Realizing that this could quickly devolve into a toxic bashing session, Chloe got straight to the point. She pitied the man but had to trust that the bartender with his keys would do the right thing when the time came.

"Mr. Hilyard, I want you to look at a picture for me and tell me if you know who it is. I believe she might have been in your graduating class."

She slid the picture over to him and he studied it hard—perhaps waiting for his vision to focus in on just the one version of the picture rather that then two or three hazy ones he was likely seeing.

"Yup. That's Melanie. Melanie Paschiutto." He then made a *pfff* sound with his lips and slapped at the picture. "Or, as everyone called her in school, Melanie Pa*shit*-o. I believe she had my lovely wife to thank for that little nickname. One of her fine contributions to high school."

"So Lauren knew her?" Chloe asked.

"Yeah, she did. Gave that poor girl hell in high school. You ever see that movie *Carrie*? The old one, not the new remade garbage. Carrie has her first period in the shower and the girls start chucking tampons at her. That's the sort of stuff Lauren did to her."

"Do you know why?"

"Other than being an evil bitch?" He frowned at this and choked back a sob. To make sure it stayed down, he gulped down some of his beer. It was getting close to empty, making him look over toward the bartender. "She wasn't like that when we got married. She got pregnant and I think she understood...started to

147

regret being so fucking mean to everyone in school. I don't know…I think she still bashed people a bit during her little porch sessions with Claire or her tea and snacks with Tabby and Kaitlin."

"Do you know *why* Lauren was so mean to this woman?"

"Because she wasn't as pretty. She was odd. A little overweight. Acne. Hand-me-down clothes. It wasn't just Lauren. Everyone picked on her. Lauren was just sort of the ringleader."

And she chose to go to her high school reunion? Chloe thought. *What the hell for?*

But she was starting to think she knew exactly why she'd gone.

"Would you happen to know where she lives?" Chloe asked.

"Melanie? No. I don't think I've spoken a word to her since high school. I think she went to community college and stuck around here, but I never spoke to her after graduation. Hell…I doubt I spoke to her at all in high school."

"Well, thank you for your time," Chloe said. She got up from her chair and saw that Rhodes was looking at Jerry Hilyard as if the sight of him was breaking her heart. Chloe turned back to him and asked: "Can we give you a ride home?"

He thought about it for a moment and then shook his head. "No. I know I'm drunk and that's okay. It's the most I've felt…the most that wasn't sorrow or pain, that is…in two weeks. And it's nice." He smiled then, a smile that made Chloe want to weep. "It's numbing. Don't give a damn about anything. I just want to drink until I pass out and it all goes black."

He looked back down into his beer before draining it and showing the empty glass to the bartender. Chloe almost tried again but left him to it. On her way out, she passed by the bartender as he took Jerry his next beer.

"Be sure you take care of him," Chloe said.

The bartender only nodded, indicating that he'd basically accepted that duty the moment the poor man had walked in. It made Chloe feel a little bit better but she realized as they walked back out to the parking lot that although she felt she was definitely on to something here, the sight of Jerry Hilyard had affected her deeply.

It made her incredibly sad, but at the same time, more determined than ever to make sure she found his wife's killer.

CHAPTER TWENTY SEVEN

It was three o'clock in the morning by the time Chloe and Rhodes had managed to get an address for one Melanie Paschiutto. The Barnes Point police department was poorly staffed at such an hour, most of the available manpower stationed on the town's many back roads to watch out for drunk drivers.

Rather than head out to speak with Melanie at such a ridiculous hour, they opted to get a room at a motel. Chloe fell asleep around 3:45, conking out the moment her head hit the bed. As was the nature of sleep, though, the final thought in her head as she drifted off followed her down and stuck to the darkness, not causing any dreams but keeping one thing in her subconscious, one thing to occupy her mind even as she slept.

It was a thought of Jacob Koontz, standing beside Kyle Moulton. It was her past, which was gone, and what she had thought might be her future, equally gone. And as that image drifted off into sleep with her, she could not help but wonder which one—the past or the future—might be more significant.

***

The alarm went off at seven o'clock. Chloe and Moulton worked well around one another as they dressed for the day. Hair and teeth brushed, somewhat energized by the three or so hours of sleep they'd had, they walked out into the morning. It was quiet and serene, Barnes Point offering a picture of its typical Sunday morning. Chloe wondered if Lauren Hilyard had experienced this on her last day alive or if she had slept through it, maybe snoozing off a few too many drinks.

As they got into the car, Chloe called Sheriff Jenkins to let him know where they were headed and some of the suspicions she had. Jenkins offered his help, stating that Jason Morton's refusal to give an admission as well as the lack of evidence was pointing to not only his release, but the eventuality of him no longer being considered the killer.

Chloe drove out to the edge of Barnes Point, taking a two-lane road that was perfectly bordered with trees that seemed to go on forever. Quaint little houses were tucked within the forest, barely visible from the road. About six miles into this repetitious scenery, they came to the address they'd found for Melanie Paschiutto the night before. There was a single car parked in the driveway. A swing set and a tattered old Little Tikes tricycle parked along the edge of the sidewalk indicated that there was at least one Paschiutto child.

They walked up to the front door, Chloe knocking lightly. Off in the distance, somewhere in the trees, birds were singing. She felt like they were in the middle of nowhere, the reality of Lauren Hilyard's death on the other side of the world.

A series of rapid footsteps came running toward the door. It opened slowly, revealing half of a small face. A little girl of about eight or so stared up at Chloe and Rhodes. When the girls realized she did not know either of these women, she stepped back and looked behind her.

"Is your mother home?" Chloe asked.

The girl nodded and yelled: "Mom! Two ladies are at the door!"

With her announcement made, she ran back into the house, leaving the door open behind her. Within seconds, a woman appeared. She was fussing with an earring as she approached the doorway.

"Can I help you?" she asked, finally getting the ring into her ear.

"Are you Melanie Paschiutto?" Chloe asked.

"Yes, that's me." She eyed them both with skepticism. Chloe watched the woman's reaction, fairly certain that was a degree of distrust in her gaze.

"Do you have a moment to talk?" Chloe asked. She showed her ID, again looking at Melanie's reaction. She was showing very little, as if she was moderately disinterested in the entire exchange.

"FBI? What's going on?"

"We're investigating the murder of Lauren Hilyard," she said. Then, stretching the truth quite a bit, she added: "We're meeting up with everyone that attended the high school reunion two weeks ago, hoping to get some answers."

She thought she saw the slightest reaction in Melanie's expression. Alarm? Caution? For a moment, she looked like a woman who had kicked over an old log and discovered a snake.

"That's fine," she said. "But I'd rather be quick about it. My daughter and I are getting ready for church."

"Of course," Chloe said as Melanie invited them in. "Hopefully, it will only take a second."

Before Melanie had even closed the door behind them, she started talking. And she spoke quickly, making it clear that she was in a hurry and wanted them out of her house as soon as possible.

"So what kind of stuff are you looking for?" she asked.

"Well, we're just getting reports from everyone in attendance, trying to find out if there was anything they saw or heard that night that might lend a clue towards why someone might want Lauren murdered."

The three of them were standing in the foyer. Apparently, Melanie was not going to invite them inside. Chloe took in the layout of the house; living room to the right, small dining room off of that, a hallway directly ahead. Melanie's daughter was currently in that hallway, skipping into the bathroom at the end of it.

"I don't recall all that much," she said. "Lauren was…well, she was not particularly nice to me in high school. So honestly, I didn't pay much attention to her at the reunion."

Lie number one, Chloe thought.

"Was there a group you stayed with that night? Anyone you might have had a conversation with?"

"No. I sort of wandered from group to group. Lots of small conversations but nothing really meaningful."

Lie number two. Why would she be lying about such a thing?

"Ms. Paschiutto, what are your memories of Lauren Hilyard in high school? How would you define her?"

Melanie took a moment before she answered. As she did, her daughter started to hum a song behind her. She was brushing her teeth in the bathroom, keeping an eye on what was transpiring in the foyer.

"She was deplorable," Melanie said. She said it with venom in her voice, as if she were talking about some inhumane crime rather than another human being. "I daresay she was evil. Just mean to everyone that didn't fit within her little circle. She…she was the type of girl I avoided at all costs."

She said all of this with a weird look of pride on her face. But that look of caution remained on her face.

"Do you think she was so mean-spirited in high school that it might have given someone reason to kill her ten years later?" Chloe asked. "Perhaps over something sparked at the reunion?"

If she had looked like a woman who had discovered a snake under a log moments ago, she now looked as if that snake had struck out at her. Her eyes went wide for a moment and she actually took a step back. She quickly regained her composure, though. Still, that split second was all Chloe had been looking for.

"I don't know. It's hard to imagine that but…well, then again, she did some pretty vile things in school."

"Like what?"

Melanie thought for a moment and then shook her head. I'm really quite sorry," she said. "But we're already running behind. I like to get Aubrey to Sunday school right when it starts at eight thirty and we're already running a little behind."

"Sure, sure," Chloe said.

"Would you call us if you think of anything else?" Rhodes asked, handing Melanie one of her business cards.

"Of course," Melanie said, the relief on her face as clear as a vibrant painting.

"Mrs. Paschiutto, I do apologize," Chloe said. "I know this seems unprofessional, but do you think I could use your restroom?"

Still overcome with relief, Melanie thought nothing of it. "No problem," she said. "Right down the hallway there and…Aubrey! Can you hop out of there for a second so this nice lady can use the restroom?"

Aubrey did as instructed. She smiled at Chloe as she dutifully stepped out of the bathroom.

"Thanks so much," Chloe said.

As she started for the restroom, directly ahead in her line of sight, she hoped that Rhodes picked up on what she was doing. Within a few seconds, it was clear that she had. Rhodes started speaking softly to Melanie—small talk, about how nice and quiet it must be out here among all of the forest.

Chloe made it to the bathroom and turned to see that Rhodes had positioned herself so that Melanie's back was turned to Chloe. As for Aubrey, she had disappeared elsewhere in the house, heading toward the kitchen.

Chloe quickly ducked into the living room area. She looked around but found the place absolutely tidy and well kept. A bible and a devotional sat on the small coffee table and a stack of kids' movies sat in a neat stack on top of the old television. She hurried out of there and went back into the hallway. When she did, she nearly collided with Aubrey. The girl waved at her and when she did, Chloe waved back. It was clear the little girl wasn't much of a talker, so Chloe risked seeming rude. She walked right past her and into the first doorway she came to along the hall.

She walked into what was obviously Melanie's bedroom. It was not nearly as clean as the living room. There were dirty clothes strewn here and there and a few books scattered on the floor. She started for the nightstand to see if there was anything to find there. It was then, passing by the books, that she stopped.

She saw the cover of one of the books on the floor. It was tattered and had clearly been used quite a bit. It was a slim book with a glossy cover. The title read: **Barnes Point High School 2009-2010.**

Sure…there was a chance that it was left over from a nostalgic trip down memory lane from having attended the reunion. Still, it seemed ominous to Chloe. She picked it up from the floor and opened it up. The first thing she noticed was that hardly anyone had signed Melanie's yearbook. There were only a handful of autographs and messages in the inside cover and most of those were from teachers.

She quickly flipped through the book, finding the senior class. She located Lauren Hilyard's photo and was not at all surprised to find devil horns and inked fire coming off of her head. Over by the listing of her name, the word **bitch** had been scrawled. She flipped through the remainder of the book and saw Lauren again, posed with a boy under a picture labeled *Most Popular*. In the picture, Lauren's eyes had been X'ed over repeatedly, so much that there were little rips in the paper. The words **PRETTY IDIOT** were scrawled across her shirt in black marker.

As she reached the end of the book, something fell out of the back. It fluttered to the floor, landing at Chloe's feet. It was an envelope, unsealed, stuffed with newspaper clippings. Chloe looked through them and found four clippings. They were all from the local paper and all about Lauren's murder.

A chill crept down Chloe's spine as she looked to the floor and saw a few more books. There were a couple of hardback novels, but she also saw two more yearbooks, both from the previous years at Barnes Point High. She found Lauren's pictures in all of them. Like the senior yearbook, all of Lauren's pictures had been defaced. In the junior yearbook, every mention or picture of Lauren had been blocked out with a steady stream of the same word: *die, die, die, die, die…*

She carried the books and newspaper clippings out of the bedroom and walked back down the hallway. Rhodes spotted her and Melanie's gaze followed. When she saw the yearbooks in her hand, Melanie's face went incredibly pale. For a moment, Chloe feared the woman was about to get sick.

"You went into my room," she said flatly.

"I did. And some of the things in these yearbooks…they're not exactly becoming of a lady that is getting dressed for church."

"You invaded my privacy…" Melanie said. Her eyes darted back and forth and her lips started to tremble as she tried to think of something else to say.

"Ms. Paschiutto…we saw video footage of the reunion," Chloe said. "You stared down Lauren Hilyard almost the entire time. And based on information we've gathered recently, we understand that she practically victimized you in high school…bullied you."

"She did. And…but…"

"It hurts to be left out," Chloe said. "It hurts even more when those that are leaving you out attack you for not being like them. It sucks to not be included…to be looked over and ignored, right?"

Melanie made a strange movement with her head then, as if she were trying to nod and shake it in a *no* gesture all at the same time. Tears started to pour from her eyes. Coupled with the angry sneer that slowly started to creep across her mouth, it was rather terrifying.

"Always looked over," she said in a hiss. "By Lauren Hilyard and her whore friends. By my own husband when he slept with every other woman in town and left me to raise this poor little girl on my own. A darling little girl that is suffering the same things I went through. Bullied and ignored. Some little shit put chocolate pudding on her cafeteria chair the other day. There's a little boy that pinches her and…"

"Ms. Paschiutto," Rhodes said slowly, calmly, "is there something you need to tell us?"

She started to breathe harder now, backing up against the wall. "It never ends," she said. "It stays in your head and it ruins your life and that bitch had the perfect life. Looks, money, a gorgeous husband that actually loved her, friends…and not a single regret about the menace she was in high school…"

Chloe felt herself tensing. Watching and listening to Melanie Paschiutto in that moment was like standing in front of a tea kettle, waiting for it to boil. Only she felt that something much worse than hot water would come out.

"Ms. Paschiutto, you can—"

"She deserved it! She deserved it and it felt…ah, God help me…"

She let out a wail as she pushed herself hard off of the wall. She came at Chloe quickly, flailing her arms as if she were being attacked by bees. She only got one swat in, trying to free the yearbooks from Chloe's hands. One of them fell to the floor but by the time she tried to swat again, Rhodes caught her flailing arm and pinned it behind her back.

Chloe stepped in to help but realized that Rhodes had it covered. When Melanie was pressed against the wall, she gave up. She sagged and started to weep as Rhodes applied the handcuffs.

A sound from behind her caused Chloe to turn. The little girl—Aubrey Paschiutto—was standing there, a hand over her mouth. It occurred to Chloe that the look on her face was more than one of bewilderment. Aubrey was recognizing something, making some connection that perhaps her little mind wasn't quite ready to handle.

"Did the prayers not work?" Aubrey asked. Her voice was tiny and constrained. She might have been on the verge of crying.

"What do you mean, sweetie?" Chloe asked.

"Don't you talk to her!" Melanie wailed. "Don't you *dare*…"

"Mom said she'd done something…something bad. A really bad sin. We prayed that God would forgive her. But…you're here for her, so I think the prayers didn't work."

Chloe had no idea how to respond to her. She placed her hand on Aubrey's shoulder and led her into the kitchen, away from the sight of her mother in handcuffs.

"Was she bad?" Aubrey asked. "Was she right? She did a very bad thing?"

"Your mom made a very bad choice," Chloe said. She wanted to say something else but couldn't find the words to explain it to such a young girl.

Instead, she pulled out her cell phone and dialed up Sheriff Jenkins as Melanie Paschiutto continued to wail and scream from the foyer.

CHAPTER TWENTY EIGHT

Everything after that happened in what felt like a whirlwind. Between finalizing things with Jenkins in Barnes Point and then making it back to DC, Chloe realized that she was both mentally and physically exhausted. The usual rush of adrenaline she felt after making a connection that closed a case wasn't there; it was replaced by uncertainty and a feeling that, even though she wrapped the case, she had somehow come out on the losing end.

Maybe it was having lost Moulton. Or maybe it was knowing that because of her so-called good work, she had left a daughter without a mother…something she knew far too much about.

Rhodes had volunteered to drive, apparently seeing the disconnected state Chloe was in. She nodded off for about ten minutes, waking up and not fully gathering where she was for a moment.

"You okay?" Rhodes asked her.

Chloe nodded. "Yeah. It's just this strange feeling of…"

Her phone rang, cutting her off. Before she grabbed it, she said a little prayer that it might be Moulton with some good news. But it was Johnson's name that was on the display. She almost ignored it but didn't see the point.

"Fine here."

"Agent Fine, I wanted you to know that I just got off of the phone with Sheriff Jenkins. It seems you left some things out of your informal debrief with me when you called earlier."

"I really don't think I did," she said. "I'll write it all up when I get home, but—"

"You're far too modest, Fine. Take the credit when it's due. He told me all about how you worked with a local DJ and video guy, looking through footage from the high school reunion. He also noted how you did this very late at night, rather than waiting. If he were single and a little younger, I'd daresay Jenkins might have a thing for you. He's over the moon about the way you handled yourself."

"Thank you, sir," Chloe said, suddenly not feeling quite as tired.

"Before you start the workday tomorrow, come by my office for a meeting with Garcia and me. We'd like to go over the case with you and talk about your future."

They set up a time for the meeting before Chloe ended the call. Rhodes looked over to her but said nothing. She, too, was tired. And if she was anything like Chloe, maybe she was also hung up on how they had nearly walked away from the case after taking in Jason Morton, so sure he had been the killer.

But even despite that corrected mistake, it was nothing compared to how Chloe was feeling about poor little Aubrey Paschiutto and how the outcome of this case would negatively impact her life.

***

"Chloe?"

Chloe opened her eyes, her heart pounding. Someone had said her name; someone was there with her. She sat up quickly, her breaths coming rapidly. Slowly, she began to understand that she had been having a dream. Nothing bad at all but certainly not a dream filled with rainbows and sunshine.

She looked toward the door to her bedroom and saw Danielle standing there. For a dizzying moment, Chloe thought she could also see Aubrey Paschiutto in the darkness. But it was just a play of shadows along the wall.

"Sorry to wake you," Danielle said. "But you sounded distressed. I know it was just a dream, but still…yikes. You sounded bad."

Chloe took a deep breath and let it out. She looked to her bedside table and saw that it was 5:35. "Did I wake you up?" Chloe asked.

"Not exactly. I haven't slept well for the last few days. Chloe…there's something on my mind and I think I need to share it with you."

"Now? At five thirty in the morning?"

"Yeah. I think so."

Chloe wiped the last remnants of the dream from her memory—a dream where Aubrey had been there every step of the way, walking right beside her as they took her mother into custody…as they showed Melanie the pictures of the Lauren Hilyard's murder scene. Of course, it had not happened like that. The Department of Social Services had come and sat with Aubrey until a next of kin could come and stay with her. It had been her uncle and as far as Chloe knew, she had remained with him in the three days that had passed since then.

"Okay," Chloe said. "Can you put the coffee on and give me a chance to get dressed?"

"Sure. But dress for a car ride. I'd like to take you somewhere if you don't mind."

"Danielle, what…"

But Danielle had already left the doorway and was headed elsewhere in the apartment. Chloe rolled out of bed and walked to the bathroom, where she threw some water in her face and brushed her teeth. While brushing, she tried to understand why those awkward fifteen minutes with Aubrey Paschiutto had affected her so much. Was it because they had arrested her mother in front of her? Was it because Melanie had insinuated that Aubrey had also been the victim of bullying even at an early age? Or was it because Aubrey had told them that her mother had confided in her, telling her that they needed to pray for forgiveness for the very thing she had done?

She wasn't sure. But she was very afraid that Aubrey's little face would be haunting her for a great deal of her life.

Chloe got dressed and walked out into the kitchen to the smell of brewing coffee. Danielle had also popped a few bagels into the toaster. She was spreading cream cheese on them as Chloe sat down at the bar.

"How far are we driving?" she asked.

"Not far. Reston."

"You want me with you to go back to your apartment?" Chloe asked.

"Something like that."

They gathered up their coffee and bagels and then headed out just twenty minutes after Chloe had gotten out of bed. They barely got ahead of Wednesday morning commuter traffic as they headed south into Virginia.

"That case really got to you, huh?" Danielle asked. She was driving, very focused on the road. She was tense, sitting upright as if awaiting some disaster.

"The case didn't. Just…the way it ended. Most cases don't end with the huge shootouts or chases like they show on TV. They just…*happen*. And when it's over, you wonder what the big deal was about. But this time…this woman's daughter. The poor thing. I just don't even know how to process what her life will be like now."

What she didn't say but was thinking, was: *The poor girl was already being teased; it's only going to get worse as she gets older and kids find out that her mother snapped and brutally murdered someone.*

They arrived in front of Danielle's apartment just after seven. Chloe noticed that Danielle was looking around right away, perhaps for any sign of Sam. But the streets were mostly quiet, disrupted by only a few people heading out for work and an older woman walking her dog.

They made their way up to Danielle's apartment. The closer they got to it, the slower Danielle seemed to move.

"I don't think he'll show up again," Chloe said, easily recalling her encounter with Sam several days ago.

"I know. But...he was right here, at this door, hammering on it like he was going to kill me." She practically jabbed her key into the lock, as if stabbing it, and opened the door.

"So what do you need to get?" Chloe asked.

"Nothing. But I need to show you something. And I'll apologize beforehand. I should have showed it to you a long time ago. But...I'm ashamed to say that I just didn't want to."

"Okay, you know how to build up suspense..."

"Hold on."

She walked to her bedroom as Chloe sat down on the couch. She listened to Danielle moving around in the room, every movement made with great care. Whatever she was getting, she was not happy about it. The tension in her posture during the drive, her build-up of small talk before getting it...she was nervous as hell.

She came back into the room with a book in her hand. It looked like a basic notebook, one of the cheap-looking standard sized ones with the black and white marbled print on the cover. Danielle sat down on the couch and handed the notebook over to Chloe.

"What's this?" Chloe asked.

Danielle sighed, unable to look Chloe in the eye when she answered. "It's Mom's journal."

For a second, Chloe felt as if someone had dropped a bomb rather than a book in her lap. She gripped it and picked it up, hesitant to open it. Of course, she was unable to help herself. She looked at the pages, all covered in her mother's slanted handwriting.

"How long have you had it?" Chloe asked.

159

"The entire time," Danielle said, wiping a tear away. "Remember when the police asked us later on if there was anything back at the house we needed? I told them to bring it to me. I knew where she kept it because I saw her putting it away one day…"

"You've had it since she died?" Chloe asked accusingly.

"I have. And like I said…I'm more sorry than you can imagine. I just…I needed something that belonged to her. And I didn't want to share it."

Honestly, Chloe knew she should be furious. But the moment in and of itself was heart-breaking. And besides that…she now had this huge piece of her mother within her reach. She thumbed through the pages and then looked at Danielle.

"And why are you showing me now?"

"When you started working towards trying to free Dad about a year ago, I almost showed it to you then. But I figured it would just make you mad. But now that he's out of prison and trying to step back into our lives like nothing happened, I thought you needed to see it."

Chloe opened it to the first page and started reading, scanning the page quickly. It felt like a private moment, and she was very aware of Danielle sitting directly beside her.

"Chloe, before you read it all, there's something you need to know. I know you never truly understood why I hate him so much. One of the reasons is easy enough to admit now that you have that journal in your hands. There was one night about a year before she died…I had a nightmare and snuck into their room. I was going to just crawl up in bed with them and nestle in, you know? But I got into the door and he was strangling her. They were standing up and he had this look in his eyes…this crazy look that, at the time, I thought made him look like a monster. And Mom's eyes were big and wide, too. She was terrified. But she saw me over his shoulder and Dad saw her looking that way. He saw me there and dropped her right away. To this day, I don't know what happened between them to make him snap like that. And neither of them pulled me to the side to talk about it. Not ever. They both just pretended that it never happened."

Chloe found herself wanting to argue against this…wanting to suggest that maybe she was still half asleep and had misunderstood what she had seen. But even in her head, Chloe realized how naïve that sounded. And the way Danielle was trembling as she told the story wasn't fake or rehearsed. It was tearing her apart to relive it.

More than that, it brought to mind the feeling of a memory that had tried to present itself earlier. An idea that there was something from their past that she was forgetting—some reason that their father had always treated Danielle different. Had it maybe been this event that had caused it?

"You said 'one of the reasons,'" Chloe said. "Are there more?"

Danielle nodded and pointed to the journal. "Yes. And they're all in there." She stood up and looked back toward her room. "I'm going to pack another bag or two for what I hope is just a temporary stay at your place. Read it. And maybe within a few pages, you'll understand even more why I never showed it to you."

Danielle walked back into her bedroom and closed the door. Chloe settled down with the notebook, her finger shaking as she opened it up again and started to read. Her mother's handwriting was very legible and neat. But that charming detail was quickly obliterated by the contents of the journal.

Within just a few lines, Chloe felt herself wanting to cry. A few more lines in, she wanted to visit her father and do to him what she had done to Sam several days ago—and maybe even worse.

It's not even sex to him anymore, but some way to control and punish me. He doesn't enjoy it unless he's hurting me.

I gained about seven pounds over the holidays and he's been calling me fat-ass for the last week. Says I look disgusting to him. Says my body has "gone to hell" ever since we had kids.

I don't think he meant to hit me the first time. I really do think he just lost control for a moment. But the second and third were intentional. I had to put a lot of makeup on this morning. Chloe even commented on it, asking if I forgot to blend it in.

Chloe was gripping the edges of the notebook tight, her teeth clenched together and her heart rampaging like a penned bull in her chest. But she could not stop reading.

I'm fairly certain he's cheating on me. He comes home smelling like perfume, but just barely...like he's tried his best to wash it off. And when I try to sleep with him, he says he's too tired or that I'm not looking good and not turning him on. He's threatened to leave me if I don't lose weight. He's started to

violently grab my breasts and the tiny little love handles I have,
reminding me of how I used to look.

He hit me again today and I blacked out for a while. He
apologized later and then went out. When he came back, he smelled
like beer and that same perfume.

He strangled me tonight. We were arguing about money and
how the girls are doing in school. I pushed up against him, arguing
my point, and he slapped me in the face. Before I knew what had
happened, he pushed me against the wall and strangled me. He said
if I ever disrespected him again, he'd kill me. He said he had
something better lined up, some better woman and some better life
and all I needed to do was give him a reason to take me out of the
picture.

She was only nine pages in by that point, but Chloe started to
feel sick to her stomach. She tossed the book on Danielle's table
and tried to stand. But her legs were wobbling. Her entire body felt
out of balance as something inside of her snapped. Some foreign
rage erupted a sob out of her that was part sorrow and part anger.

Slowly, Danielle opened the bedroom door and peered in at
her. "You okay?"

"No," she said in a groan of rage. "Danielle...you should have
showed me this sooner."

"I know. I'm sorry and—"

"I helped free him and...he..."

"I know," Danielle said.

Chloe finally managed to get to her feet. She picked the
notebook back up and held it gently, as if it might be poisonous.

"I was wrong from the start," Chloe said. "My doubts...my
hopes that he was a good man. Everything..."

It all settled into her head then. The logic and truth of it. A truth
she had not only denied most of her life but one she had recently
worked to falsify. As it settled on her, she spoke it into being, made
herself listen to the words coming out of her own mouth.

"He did it," she said. Her tone was stern and confident and
barbed with anger. "It was him all along. He killed our mother."

With that stark realization, another one came to her. This one
helped to calm her, to even make her wonder if his freedom might
play in her favor.

And now the bastard is out of prison. So if I go after him, he won't have the penal system or a jail cell to protect him.

SILENT NEIGHBOR
(A Chloe Fine Psychological Suspense Mystery—Book 4)

"A masterpiece of thriller and mystery. Blake Pierce did a magnificent job developing characters with a psychological side so well described that we feel inside their minds, follow their fears and cheer for their success. Full of twists, this book will keep you awake until the turn of the last page."
--Books and Movie Reviews, Roberto Mattos (re Once Gone)

SILENT NEIGHBOR (A Chloe Fine Mystery) is book #4 in a new psychological suspense series by bestselling author Blake Pierce, whose #1 bestseller Once Gone (Book #1) (a free download) has over 1,000 five-star reviews.

When a flashy, new neighbor flaunts her wealth in a suburban town, it isn't long before she's found murdered. Did her flaunting ways upset her envious neighbors?

Or was there a deeper secret to her husband's fortune?

FBI VICAP Special Agent Chloe Fine, 27, finds herself immersed in a small-town world of lies, cliques, gossip and betrayal as she tries to separate truth from lies.

But what is the real truth?

And can she solve it while also dealing with the release of her troubled father from jail, and the spiraling down of her troubled sister?

An emotionally wrought psychological suspense with layered characters, small-town ambiance and heart-pounding suspense, THE SILENT NEIGHBOR is book #4 in a riveting new series that will leave you turning pages late into the night.

Book #5 in the CHLOE FINE series will be available soon.

Blake Pierce

Blake Pierce is author of the bestselling RILEY PAGE mystery series, which includes fourteen books (and counting). Blake Pierce is also the author of the MACKENZIE WHITE mystery series, comprising eleven books (and counting); of the AVERY BLACK mystery series, comprising six books; of the KERI LOCKE mystery series, comprising five books; of the MAKING OF RILEY PAIGE mystery series, comprising four books (and counting); of the KATE WISE mystery series, comprising five books (and counting); of the CHLOE FINE psychological suspense mystery, comprising four books (and counting); and of the JESSE HUNT psychological suspense thriller series, comprising four books (and counting).

An avid reader and lifelong fan of the mystery and thriller genres, Blake loves to hear from you, so please feel free to visit www.blakepierceauthor.com to learn more and stay in touch.

BOOKS BY BLAKE PIERCE

A JESSIE HUNT PSYCHOLOGICAL SUSPENSE SERIES
THE PERFECT WIFE (Book #1)
THE PERFECT BLOCK (Book #2)
THE PERFECT HOUSE (Book #3)

CHLOE FINE PSYCHOLOGICAL SUSPENSE SERIES
NEXT DOOR (Book #1)
A NEIGHBOR'S LIE (Book #2)
CUL DE SAC (Book #3)

KATE WISE MYSTERY SERIES
IF SHE KNEW (Book #1)
IF SHE SAW (Book #2)

THE MAKING OF RILEY PAIGE SERIES
WATCHING (Book #1)
WAITING (Book #2)
LURING (Book #3)

RILEY PAIGE MYSTERY SERIES
ONCE GONE (Book #1)
ONCE TAKEN (Book #2)
ONCE CRAVED (Book #3)
ONCE LURED (Book #4)
ONCE HUNTED (Book #5)
ONCE PINED (Book #6)
ONCE FORSAKEN (Book #7)
ONCE COLD (Book #8)
ONCE STALKED (Book #9)
ONCE LOST (Book #10)
ONCE BURIED (Book #11)
ONCE BOUND (Book #12)
ONCE TRAPPED (Book #13)
ONCE DORMANT (book #14)

MACKENZIE WHITE MYSTERY SERIES
BEFORE HE KILLS (Book #1)
BEFORE HE SEES (Book #2)
BEFORE HE COVETS (Book #3)

BEFORE HE TAKES (Book #4)
BEFORE HE NEEDS (Book #5)
BEFORE HE FEELS (Book #6)
BEFORE HE SINS (Book #7)
BEFORE HE HUNTS (Book #8)
BEFORE HE PREYS (Book #9)
BEFORE HE LONGS (Book #10)
BEFORE HE LAPSES (Book #11)

AVERY BLACK MYSTERY SERIES
CAUSE TO KILL (Book #1)
CAUSE TO RUN (Book #2)
CAUSE TO HIDE (Book #3)
CAUSE TO FEAR (Book #4)
CAUSE TO SAVE (Book #5)
CAUSE TO DREAD (Book #6)

KERI LOCKE MYSTERY SERIES
A TRACE OF DEATH (Book #1)
A TRACE OF MUDER (Book #2)
A TRACE OF VICE (Book #3)
A TRACE OF CRIME (Book #4)
A TRACE OF HOPE (Book #5)

CPSIA information can be obtained
at www.ICGtesting.com
Printed in the USA
LVHW032228031019
633101LV00013B/674